LEGACY

LEGACY

CHRIS COPPEL

Matador
9 Priory Business Park,
Wistow Road, Kibworth Beauchamp,
Leicestershire. LE8 0RX
Tel: 0116 279 2299
Email: books@troubador.co.uk
Web: www.troubador.co.uk/matador
Twitter: @matadorbooks

ISBN 978 1800462 304

British Library Cataloguing in Publication Data.
A catalogue record for this book is available from the British Library.

Printed and bound in Great Britain by 4edge Limited
Typeset in 11pt Minion Pro by Troubador Publishing Ltd, Leicester, UK

Matador is an imprint of Troubador Publishing Ltd

CHAPTER
ONE

She sat in the pitch-dark trying to expend as little energy as possible. She was very weak. She had almost left it too long this time. She had allowed her life force to wane dangerously. She had permitted too much time to pass since her last feeding. She knew that she had to feed the light at least every quarter century for her to continue her existence, even when not in human form. Despite spending most of her time in the alternate realm where her spirit didn't need to take on the appearance of a solid shape, she still expended energy. To feed the light, she knew she had to again take on her original mortal form, even though it was now so ancient and decrepit she hated every second spent within its aged confines. She wished that her powers had given her the ability to occupy the youthful bodies of her bloodline once she had taken their life force, but she had never been granted that level of physical dominance.

From her lair outside her original dimension, she had seen time pass like no one else on earth. When the last of her kind were being hunted and burned alive at the stake, she had managed to evade her pursuers. Instead of running and hiding, she used the powers with which she'd been blessed to not just evade the hunters, but to move between the realms. The magic had come, as great things often do, at a great cost. Her ability to travel outside the laws of physics required unbelievable sacrifice, both by her and by those on which she had to prey.

Despite her immense knowledge and magical abilities, when she first used her powers to move between realms she had never anticipated that with each feeding she would gain not just the light, but twenty-five living years from each donor. She had fed the light fourteen times starting in 1643 when she was only twenty-eight years old. She had witnessed almost 400 years of change in the old realm. She'd seen plague, war and famine repeat itself over and over again. She'd watched sleepy towns grow from walled enclaves to sprawling cities of glass and steel. She'd seen the first train, the first aircraft and even the first rocket blast its way off the planet.

None of that mattered to her in the least. The days when she cared about what went on within the old realm were long gone. Centuries gone. She now had only one focus.

To follow her bloodline and feed the light.

CHAPTER
TWO

The banging on the door shook the entire house. Craig had been prepared to ignore the 2am disturbance and continue with the X-rated dream he'd been having. His wife, Jenny, however, had no intention of letting that happen and neither did Steeler, their oversized yellow lab. He was barking up a storm somewhere downstairs.

"Aren't you going to see who it is?" Jenny mumbled.

"At this time of the morning, I don't care."

The banging repeated. This time it was even louder, sending Steeler into an even more intense barking jag. They heard Sally, their four-year-old, start crying in her bedroom just across the hall. Tim, their five-year-old, then came moping into the room and jumped on the bed.

"Mommy, what's that noise? Please make it stop," he pleaded.

"Daddy is going to go down right now and make it go away. Aren't you, sweetheart?"

Craig fumbled to turn on his bedside light. Though thirty-seven, he could still pass for being in his mid to late twenties. He exercised daily and tried hard to keep himself in good shape – more for work purposes than vanity. He ran his hands through his sandy blonde hair then reluctantly swung his legs off the warm and comfy memory-foam bed and forced his feet into his threadbare slippers. Jenny had tried, on numerous occasions, to buy replacement footwear, but he always went back to the same pair he'd worn for twelve years.

Craig grabbed his terrycloth robe off the back of the door.

"Will you go and try to get Sally settled while I find out what idiot is trying to smash down our door?" Craig said.

Tim immediately looked scared. "Somebody is smashing down our door?"

Jenny glared at Craig for his poor choice of words.

He pulled a 'whoops' face then headed down the narrow stairway. He bundled the robe more tightly around himself in an attempt to ward of the chill from the old house. In an effort to cut down on the utility bills, they kept the heating off overnight. As they were usually tucked up under layers of quilted covers they didn't feel the wrath of the high desert winter cold. The downside to the cost savings was that any time spent out of the bed during the night hours was brutal. A trip all the way to the front door was really going to take a toll.

Just as Craig reached the tiny hallway at the bottom of the stairs, Steeler ran up to him, head-butted his thigh then started the crazy sideways dance he did whenever he got over excited.

Another volley of percussive banging on the house's wooden front door seemed to shake the whole building to its foundation. Craig was surprised the door hadn't splintered in two after the repeated abuse. Then again, Craig realised, the door had lasted close to 150 years so some asshole's knuckles were unlikely to finish it off at this point.

He stopped and opened the hall cupboard then entered the six-digit code into the gun safe bolted to the wall. He removed his police issue Glock 19, slipped in a fresh clip and chambered a round. He held the gun calmly at his side.

He reached the front door and checked the peephole. As usual he could hardly see a thing. It pissed him off that he kept procrastinating about getting either a peephole that actually worked or maybe even something a little more high tech like a Ring camera doorbell. Of course, it didn't help him at that moment.

"I am going to open the door now," Craig shouted. "I am a sheriff's deputy and I am armed. Please step back and keep your hands in view."

He waited a few seconds then undid the old-fashioned lock as well as the more modern deadbolt. He threw open the door, ready for a confrontation. The sub-zero blast of air hit him like a fist. The first thing he saw were the tail lights of a grey truck bumping its way along their snow-covered gravel drive. It was hard to tell in the dark, but he got the impression that it was a very old vehicle.

The second thing he saw was the box.

It was huge. Craig was a big guy and the box was taller than him. It was at least six and a half feet high, three feet wide and about one and a half feet deep. It was covered in heavy-duty brown wrapping paper. A small label was in the geometric centre of the package.

It read: *TO THE EDMONDS FAMILY.*

There was no other information. No address, no mention of who sent it or even which courier company had delivered it. That was the biggest disappointment, as Craig desperately wanted to give them a call in the morning and give them a little piece of his mind concerning middle-of-the-night deliveries.

Craig considered leaving the box outside, but it had clearly snowed earlier and would most likely do so again. He had no idea what was in the thing but doubted that a good beating by a winter storm would do it much good.

He knew just by looking at it that it was going to be a battle to get it through the old doorway. He deduced that the only way to get the box inside was to tip it on its side then drag it into the hallway while lifting it back to its full height once inside.

As he tilted it, he suddenly realised that it was extremely heavy and solid. He had to use every ounce of his strength to not let the top end crash down onto the brick entry.

He manhandled the brown monolith-like package through the entryway and onto the flagstone-floored hallway. After securely locking the front door, he turned back to the mystery box wondering if he should check its contents there and then or wait till morning.

The decision was made for him as Jenny called down from upstairs.

"Who was it?"

"I think it was a courier. Someone has sent us a giant box. I was just thinking of opening it."

"You'll do no such thing. You must be freezing and the kids aren't going to calm down until you're back up here where you belong."

"You're the one who made me get out of bed and come down here," Craig shot back.

Jenny used her ultra-calm voice. The one that left no room for misinterpretation. "Come back to bed, please. You can open your box in the morning."

Craig gave the box one last glance before returning the gun to its locker and heading back up to their warm bed.

Craig woke as he usually did, to the dawn chorus of breakfast-making and children waking. Before the kids, the transition from sleep to being fully awake had been a gradual and peaceful experience. Now it was like jumping onto a moving roller coaster in mid-ride. You just had to hang on and hope for the best.

It was Saturday and he didn't have a shift till the next day, so he at least didn't need to battle for his place in the bathroom queue. The little house had been his and Jenny's dream. The kids had been another, but staggered aspect of the same fantasy. The house was indescribably quaint. Having been built in the late 1800s by an early settler to Southern Utah, it was not exactly stuffed full of all the mod cons. Despite that, they'd fallen in love with it the moment they saw it. It was perfect. It had privacy. It sat on ten acres that butted up against BLM (Bureau of Land Management) property. It had been plenty big enough for the two of them and they had hoped it would even suit their needs when the time came to start a family.

Kids had arrived and it soon became apparent that the house wasn't big enough, yet they simply couldn't bring themselves to give up all the positives just for the efficiency of having a little extra space.

The one aspect that they'd never fully fleshed out in their master plan was what the impact would be of four people living life to the fullest within the confines of a 1200-square-foot house. Especially when two of them were very small and very messy people who seemed to constantly need to use the one and only bathroom for purposes far beyond those for which the room had originally been intended.

They'd applied to Kane County for a permit to extend the back of the house by adding an extra bedroom and family bathroom. They were granted approval but it came with a condition. The property's sewage waste fed into a pre-existing leach field. As long as the home was in its original condition, the approval of use for this archaic system was grandfathered to the owner. If they were going to structurally remodel, especially if that included the addition of a toilet, they would have to install a modern septic tank.

Craig tried to argue the point that someone at some time in the past had already screwed up the original purity of the home by installing indoor plumbing, electricity and an upstairs bathroom. He suggested they reconsider his planning request on the basis of there already having been a precedent for improvement.

The county rejected his request adding that, as their home was considered an historic building because of its age, he was lucky they didn't require him to convert the house back to its original condition *sans* the luxury of plumbing, heat and electricity.

Craig decided that there were some battles that one just knew couldn't be won. They'd also known before they bought the house that any remodelling would probably come with some costly conditions.

Craig had assumed that a septic tank couldn't be that expensive. He was wrong. The cost to install one almost doubled the estimated cost for the whole extension.

And so, the family persevered.

Craig threw on a pair of jeans and a T-shirt then checked the bathroom before heading downstairs. He was amazed to find it vacant though it did look as though a tornado had recently passed through. Even though years had passed since the patter of little feet became the normal background track to his life, Craig was still amazed at how many towels two children could use for one pre-breakfast face wash. He counted seven.

Jenny enforced a strict 'don't just leave things on the floor' policy so each towel had been draped over something.

Strangely none of the hooks or racks that were there for just such a purpose were rarely, if ever considered. One towel was thrown over the toilet seat, another hung from the washbasin's hot tap and another was stuffed through the horizontal blinds.

Craig felt pretty certain that each of the chosen towel-hanging places had to have been much harder to coordinate than placing them where they were supposed to go. Then again, Craig no longer thought with that freedom of disconnected thought with which a child's mind is blessed.

As he hung a few up just to have them out of the way, he noticed that they were beyond soaking wet. How could anyone, even a small child, drench towel after towel when carrying out something so basic as giving their face a quick wash.

"Don't dawdle in there too long," Jenny called. "Breakfast is ready and the kids want to open the big present."

"Be right down."

Craig had actually forgotten about the big box he'd battled with earlier in the morning as he was still half asleep and hadn't had any coffee yet.

Craig quickly finished his post-wake-up toiletries then headed downstairs. The box was still in the hallway and he saw that part of the brown paper appeared to have been peeled away already. Judging by the small width of the rips, hands of the little people had unquestioningly been involved.

"I see that some field mice have been at the package already," he declared as he walked into the kitchen.

"NOOO, Daddy. It wasn't mice. It was us. We wanted

to surprise you, but then Mommy said we had to wait for you before we could open it," Sally exclaimed.

Craig grinned at the sight of his family all gathered in the kitchen. Even Steeler was lying belly up on the tile floor waiting for either a tummy rub or an errant scrap to fall from the counter.

Jenny was wearing a pair of work jeans and one of his old shirts. She hadn't put on any make-up yet and her blonde hair was pulled back into a simple ponytail. She looked stunningly beautiful.

They had met when Craig was on leave in San Diego and Jenny had been attending a graphic artists convention off campus. Somehow they ended up in the same bar in the Gaslamp Quarter. She was with fellow students from UCSD and he, with some of his Marine buddies.

In retrospect, Craig realised that it may not have been the most auspicious start to a romance but somehow it had worked out for them.

Craig looked over at his children. Tim was engrossed in a puzzle on the back of his cinnamon cereal box. Sally had obviously started her day with a nutritious bowl of Fruit Loops judging by the pink-coloured milk remnants in her bowl. Jenny had waited for Craig to appear before depositing a plate of scrambled eggs with a side of wholegrain toast at the head of the table.

"Thanks, babe." He gave her a peck on the cheek as he sat down.

Jenny's final task before getting to enjoy her own breakfast was to place Craig's oversized coffee mug in front of him. It had been given to him as a birthday present by his fellow officers at the Kanab sheriff's department. It read 'To Provide and Be Served'.

Craig ate his food as he listened to Sally tell a lengthy saga about a moth that had got stuck in her room the previous day. The story lasted through the eggs and two cups of coffee. Finally, with everyone fed, watered and up to date on the moth adventures, they could all focus on the big event.

Unwrapping the big box.

CHAPTER
THREE

"Right!" Craig announced. "The first thing is to get this mother…"

"Craig!" Jenny scolded as she leant her head towards the children. "Sorry. The first thing is to get this… thing into the living room so we have some room to work. Jen, could you get me a couple of dry towels so we can shove one under each end? I think that once we get it onto carpet we'll be fine, but we've got to get it out of the hall first."

Jenny went into the narrow utility room off the kitchen and reappeared a few moments later with two of their shabbier towels that had been relegated to domestic spills and the like.

Craig took each one and folded it lengthwise until he had a narrow towel strip that he could force under each end of the monster. He and Jenny then took a side of the box and grabbed a towel end in each hand.

Tim was assigned the vital task of being the traffic controller.

Sally was on her hands and knees staring at a bug so was able to shirk the workload entirely. Steeler had been released into the wild so he could chase the wild bunnies and turkeys – neither of which did he ever even come close to catching.

With Tim giving the all clear for traffic heading towards the living room, Jenny and Craig began sliding the thing inch by inch along the flagstone flooring. It took almost five minutes of straining and micro movements, but they finally reached the demarcation line between the hard stone and the soft, forgiving carpet of the living room. Craig had been right. The monster box slid almost effortlessly across the surface of the carpetting.

Once they'd moved it into the centre of the room. Craig and Jenny carefully laid it flat with the label facing up. After a bit of post-exertion stretching, the four attacked the brown paper. They ripped most of it off in record time. There was still some on the underside, but they had no need (or way) of removing that.

Once the paper was gone they could see why the thing was so heavy. They had unearthed an industrial quality-pine packing crate. Craig had to retrieve his tool bag from the utility room as the top was held on with over a dozen serious-looking screws.

It took almost an hour of unexpected effort and metal against wood squealing to get them out. Once done, Craig tried to lift off the crate lid. It didn't budge.

He stared at Jenny. "This better not be some sort of prank."

"I'm sure it's not, but even if it is, so what? We're enjoying it, aren't we?" She turned to Sally who wasn't paying any attention to the box any more. She was making little paper origami sculptures from the brown wrapping. Tim had also lost interest and was using a large piece of the wrapping paper as a cape and was busy battling an invisible adversary.

"Who are you today?" Jenny asked.

"I'm Batman and I'm fighting the bad guys!"

"Well, please don't break anything."

Craig used his biggest flat-head screwdriver and began forcing it under the lid and prying it upwards.

"Why is the wood screaming?" Sally asked after an especially loud squeal. "Is Daddy hurting it?"

Jenny laughed as she explained that it was just the sound that wood made when it rubbed against other wood. Sally did not look at all convinced by the answer.

Craig finally managed to lever one edge up and was able, with a little help from his trusty crowbar, to manhandle the top off the base. Another layer of brown wrapping paper greeted them. Whatever it concealed had been fastidiously packed. Even the crate looked to be a custom job.

They could see that the item was the same approximate shape as the crate, but obviously slightly smaller. Craig and Jenny carefully lifted the object out of its protective shelter and laid it next to the crate.

Sally had the honour of ripping off the first swath of paper. Under that they saw an extra layer of corrugated cardboard.

Craig'd had enough. He pulled his utility knife from his side pocket and with care to not pierce himself or the enshrouded mystery object, he sliced through the paper and cardboard from one end to the other.

As he parted the last vestige of protection, the mystery article was revealed.

"That's not something fun!" Sally stated with exaggerated disappointment before stomping out of the room.

"I have to agree with her," Craig said.

"There's something wrong with both of you. It's beautiful," Jenny voiced.

They stared down at the mirror within its carved wooden frame with curiosity and just the slightest sense of unexplained concern.

"Booooring!" Tim offered as he stopped his great battle to have a look.

"Let's get it out of the box," Jenny grinned.

Together, Craig and Jenny lifted it out of the coffin-like crate and leaned it against the wall. Jenny stood back to get a better view of the thing. She tugged Craig back by his T-shirt to join her.

It was quite something. It was obviously old. Very old. The mirror had yellowed with time and was pitted. It had backing missing along most of its edging and a small crack across the top right-hand corner. All in all, it wasn't in great shape.

The frame however was the kicker. It appeared to be hand carved from what Craig guessed was walnut. The carving was almost simplistic and seemed to depict forest animals amid leafy foliage. For some reason the carving was only on the sides and top panel of the frame. The bottom section was much narrower and was completely plain. It certainly wasn't the work of an artisan yet there was something intrinsically beautiful about its artistic naivety. The more Craig looked at the carvings the more detail he seemed to perceive.

"It's so unusual," Jenny said. "I wonder who made it? It looks really old."

"You're the one who's plugged into all those reference sites that show historical designs back to whenever. You should check it out."

"The sites I use show the history of graphic design not wood carving."

"I'm sure there's a correlation there somewhere," Craig suggested.

"Spoken like a true cop," Jenny replied.

"The bigger question is, who the heck sent it to us?"

"And why?" Jenny added. "It looks like it could be valuable."

"Want to pack it back up again and stick it in the workshop?"

"Absolutely not. Until we find out that this has all been a terrible mistake, I want it up on the wall," she insisted. "In fact, right there. We've been wondering what to do with that space for ages."

Jenny pointed at a section of bare wall just to the left of the archway between the hallway and the living room. Craig retrieved a laser measure from his tool bag and took a couple of readings.

"It would fit. What are you thinking – halfway up the wall?" Craig asked.

Jenny was staring at it closely. "Actually, no. I think it's meant to look like a doorway. That's why the bottom is unadorned. It should be hung with that section just touching the floor."

"Unadorned? Is that your special word for the day?" Craig teased.

"Read a little. You'd be amazed. You'd learn lots of new words, maybe even big ones." She gave him a snarky grin.

"Let's see what it looks like." Jenny took hold of the left side of the mirror and waited for Craig to grab the other side.

"You sure you want it in here? There's something creepy about it, plus it's not ours."

"It must be. It was addressed to us," Jenny said.

"Actually, there was no address on the label, just our name. There's probably thousands of Edmonds in Utah."

"Then why was it dropped off here?"

"I have no idea. I was thinking that when I get to work tomorrow, I can check some of the camera feeds on 89. Maybe I can get the licence number off the truck and track down who delivered it," Craig suggested.

"Sounds like a plan. In the meantime, let's see what it looks like on the wall. Pleeeease."

"Jeez. What a whiner," he joked. "Okay. Get a good grip and we'll lift in three. One… two… three."

They raised the mirror and though heavy, it was nothing compared to the weight of it when it was still in its crate. They carried it across the room and leaned it where Jenny had suggested.

"Wow," Craig sounded surprised. "It actually looks pretty good there."

Jenny stepped back to get a better perspective of the entire area.

"Everything all right?" Craig asked.

"Yes. It's just... it looks perfect there. Maybe even too perfect."

"Too perfect? What does that mean?"

"It looks like it completely belongs there. Almost like it's always belonged there," she replied.

"Is that a bad thing?"

Jenny forced a smile. "I sure hope not."

"We still have the option of the workshop," he reminded her.

"Don't be ridiculous. I'm just being silly. It looks fantastic there. It actually pulls the whole room together," Jenny stated.

"So, it stays?" he asked.

"Yes. It stays."

Craig sighed.

CHAPTER
FOUR

After packing up all the wrapping paper and hauling the crate out to the back of the workshop, the Edmonds returned to their normal Saturday routine.

The adults got their fifteen minutes each of bathroom time (the kids would be bathed later in the evening). There needed to be constant rationing as the water heater had been playing up for a few weeks, resulting in short bursts of hot and longer bursts of tepid water interspersed with the occasional freezing cold deluge that sent the recipient scurrying out of the shower.

Jenny gave her shopping list one final check then reviewed her family's attire making sure that everyone was bundled up appropriately for the bitter cold. After ensuring that Steeler was in the utility room, safe and warm, they headed out.

Normally they would have taken Jenny's Ford Escape but after the recent snow and the sub-zero temperatures, they felt a four-wheel drive was the better bet. The only downside with taking Craig's Explorer was that it was a sheriff's vehicle complete with signage and a light bar on top. It certainly wasn't a subtle way to drive into town, but it was a damn sight safer than two-wheel drive.

They piled into the SUV and were about to leave when Jenny suddenly ran back to the house and locked the front door. Her family looked at her like she'd lost her mind.

"What?" she stared back at them. "We don't have any idea of the value of that mirror or why it was left with us. I'd just feel safer if we locked the house when we are out."

The fact was that they'd never locked their house once in the ten years they'd owned it. No one in Johnson Canyon locked anything. There was nobody around to steal anything. Besides everyone knew everyone and would immediately question a stranger even if you weren't home. Then there was the fact that folks in the canyon had a love for guns. Every home in the canyon was better armed than a presidential security detail.

As they drove down their drive, Craig looked back in the mirror as he often did and felt a sense of pride at their bright yellow two-storey home. It really was a home. The first one he'd ever known as an adult.

Craig sometimes, no, make that most times, wondered how the hell he'd ever made it this far.

He'd been born in Arizona in the small town of Apache Junction. It was nestled under the shadow of the infamous Superstition Mountains. They had earned that name through Native American lore and a belief by many that a fortune in gold was still waiting to be found somewhere in the rugged hills in the 'lost Dutchman' mine. In reality the only thing buried up there were the dreams of countless prospectors who had dug till they died looking for an easy way out.

Craig's dad was a door-to-door salesman at a time when few still existed and even fewer still could make any sort of a living ringing doorbells. He liked to call himself a sales executive, but the fact was that he just went from house to house, day in and day out, with his little plastic display case showing a cross-section of a couple of different styles of Excelsior-brand double-glazed windows.

There had been a time when he actually used to take quite a few orders. He'd come home with a big smile on his face, a bunch of flowers in one hand and a bottle of fancy wine in the other.

Craig couldn't remember exactly when that 'good period' ended but he knew it had been going bad for a while. His dad would come home without the smile and without the flowers, but he still had one hand around the neck of a bottle. The problem was that the bottles seemed to get bigger in direct proportion to how bad his day had been and that in turn related directly to how much his folks would fight when he'd gone to bed.

By the time the bottles became jugs, his dad stopped spending as much time on the road and his mom spent less time cleaning and cooking. The only thing they always found time for was to scream obscenities at each other not long after Craig had put himself to bed. Craig would listen until he could hear one or both of his parents start to cry. That was a good sign. That meant they were done fighting for the night and some semblance of peace would again descend on their little house.

Once summer hit, there were fewer and fewer moments of peace in their home. After an exceptionally hot August day punctuated by a fierce monsoonal thunderstorm, his folks went at it with extra gusto. With percussive thunder tailing the forked lightning with less than a one second interval, Craig knew that the storm was right above him. Both storms were right above him. One outside, one in.

The storm finally seemed about to move further down the valley when Craig heard another sharp crack of thunder then, a few moments later, a second one. He thought it strange that he hadn't actually seen the lightning but then, desert weather was always pretty weird.

The next morning, Craig came downstairs expecting to smell the coffee brewing. Something about the jug of wine seemed to make his folks gulp the stuff down. Not that morning. There was no coffee dripping into the hard-water-stained pot. There was also no cereal or milk on the dining table.

He had never had to make his own breakfast before but pouring some milk over some generic multicoloured hoops was hardly that big of a challenge.

He ate his cereal in silence. He wanted to turn on their old jumbo TV to watch cartoons but for some reason felt that on that morning, his folks should be left in peace.

He found stuff to do both inside and outside in their chain-link fenced yard that the desert sun had scorched into a barren dirt rectangle. After a few hours something told him that maybe he should check on his parents. Since the jugs started arriving they had often come downstairs looking pretty sick but they had at least always come down the stairs.

He tried to avoid the squeaky parts of the staircase as he climbed it. He didn't want to disturb them if they were sleeping. He wasn't surprised to see that their bedroom door was closed as usual. When he was younger, when the flowers still made an appearance, he would knock and they would often as not let him in. Since the jug, they either wouldn't respond or if they did it was to tell him to go away and leave them be.

He tried knocking but no one answered. He decided that they must be sleeping longer that day so he went back downstairs and played with his Lego set.

By midday, he was starting to get a little worried. He knew how to make breakfast but lunch was a whole different matter. It involved glass jars for the peanut butter and the jelly and even a knife for cutting the bread. He knew he wasn't allowed to do any of the tasks involved with lunch.

He decided to try their door one more time. Again, nobody responded to his knocking. He thought of opening it, but without permission he just didn't want to chance it. He would always remember the angry looks on their faces the last time he'd done it, but it was the spanking he got that would live forever in some dark corner of his memory.

He unconsciously rubbed his right cheek as he stepped away from the door. As he climbed down the stairs a thought struck him. A crazy thought. What if they weren't in the room at all? What if they'd just upped and left him? They hadn't seemed happy for a while. Maybe it was something he had done. Maybe they decided to run away and be happy somewhere else without him.

Craig ran down the stairs and out the front door. He immediately saw that their car was right where it was supposed to be, under the corrugated tin carport. He'd never been so happy to see the ugly brown Chevy Nova. Craig sat on the front steps waiting for something. He didn't know what, but he somehow knew he had to wait. He was really hungry and could almost taste the PB&J sandwich that had become his lunchtime staple. The nucleus of an idea started to form in his young mind. What if he just had more cereal for lunch instead of a sandwich? He'd never done that before or even seen anyone do it but, surely when you're really hungry, exceptions can be made.

It took him another thirty minutes of deep deliberation before he finally decided that the time had come for action. He wasn't sure what trouble he might be in for having cereal twice in a day. He didn't even know if his young stomach would tolerate it. It could be like the time he snuck a second piece of cheesecake and had hurled till he could only bring up bubbly yellow foam.

Craig started to get to his feet when he heard a vehicle on the dirt road that served their house and twelve others on the poorly maintained cul-de-sac. It was still out of sight but no one could mistake the sound of that untuned, misfiring engine. He stepped out onto the cracked and weed-riddled driveway and saw the old white converted van with USPS stencilled on the side. It was the mailman. He usually left their letters and fliers in their box at the communal mail drop at the end of the road but if he had something bigger or something that needed signing for, he'd come right up to the house.

Craig stepped back to allow the van to pull up front. Danny Berrick took a moment to find something in the back of the vehicle then wound his window down. He held a brown wrapped box out to Craig.

"Can I just hand this to you?" he asked in his usual scratchy voice before noticing that Craig looked both miserable and overheated. "You okay there, champ?"

Craig liked being called champ, even though he'd never actually earned the title.

"I'm hungry and Mommy and Daddy won't come downstairs," Craig blurted out.

"Where are they?"

"In their bedroom, I think. I looked everywhere else. I don't think they ran away."

Danny tried not to show his concern. Everyone in town knew about the kid's parents and their drinking and fighting.

"Can you please knock on their door?" Craig asked, almost pleadingly. "If I do it again I might get in trouble."

Danny slowly stepped out of the van. He wasn't sure what the rule book had to say about what he was about to do, but he couldn't leave the little guy waiting outside in the heat. There was also the slight problem of him being on the register. He should never have been added to it in the first place. Lord all mighty, all he'd done was go to second base with his girlfriend a heap o' years ago. He was sixteen at the time and she was fifteen. She wanted to fool around as much as he did. She'd then boasted about the encounter to her best friend who for some reason decided to mention it to her mom, and bingo! Danny became a registered sex offender for the rest of his life.

The fact that he'd remained with that girlfriend, who was now his wife and had borne him a house full of little ones, didn't seem to matter in the eyes of the law. He had to consider everything he did both outside and even inside his own home. Wrestling with your kids might be considered perfectly acceptable for most fathers. It wasn't considered right at all for someone who had his name on the list. The only reason he'd got the post office job was because his uncle was the postmaster in Apache Junction and knew that though he was on the list, there was no one alive less likely to harm a child than Danny.

"I'll tell you what, champ. You stay out here on the stoop while I have a quick look inside. You okay with that?"

Craig nodded.

"I've never been in your house so could you please tell me which room is theirs?" Danny asked.

Craig did better than that. He pointed up to a window facing the driveway. It was half open and the old faded yellow mini blinds were wafting back and forth within the frame.

"Got it. I'll just be a minute."

Danny stepped into the house.

He was gone a lot longer than a minute.

He made his way up the stairs and to the end of the short hallway. He took a moment before knocking on the door. Something wasn't right. He didn't consider himself as having a sixth sense or whatever but sometimes you could feel something just wasn't quite right. This was one of those times. The hairs on the back of his neck were standing straight out. Nope. Things were not right at all.

As he brought his hand up to knock, the door moved slightly in its jam. Probably because of the open window.

The thing was that Danny could feel a slight whisper of air move past the ill-fitting door and out into the hallway. It carried a sour scent that shouldn't have been there. It was faint but still hard to miss. He delivered to plenty of houses and was used to all the different smells, some clean some not, but this one had nothing to do with cleanliness.

Danny knocked then listened with his ear against the door. He heard nothing.

"Mr Winchell – Mrs Winchell, it's Danny Berrick from the post office."

He followed his announcement with another, harder knock. Still no response. Danny grasped the cheap ceramic doorknob and tried to turn it. It didn't budge.

He no longer had the slight sense something was wrong. By that point every alarm in his system was glowing red and ringing bells. He retrieved his wallet and decided that his laminated library card was probably the best tool for the job.

He dropped to one knee and peered between the jam and the door right where the handle was. He could clearly see the worn metal tongue with its curved side facing out. Danny pushed his library card against the curved metal, forcing it back into the lock mechanism.

The door opened on squeaky hinges while he was still taking a knee. The bed was on the right but from his angle he couldn't see what was on it. He could however pick up that scent that had seemed subtle on the other side of the door. It wasn't subtle any more.

Danny slowly stood and stepped fully into the room.

As he feared, they were both dead. A Ruger 38 revolver was on the bed between them. Danny wasn't a policeman and didn't know the first thing about forensics, other than what he'd seen on TV, but it didn't take Sherlock Holmes to work out that they'd both been shot. Her in the left temple, him straight up through his chin.

If he'd had to guess, he would have said that he shot her first as she was lying flat with her head still on the pillow whereas he looked to have been sitting upright when he fired into his head. His body had slumped over to the right with his head resting on the nightstand.

The centre of the bed was pretty much blood free. The same could not be said for the left and right side of the old Comfort Sleeper, the nightstands and the wall behind where the man's head had been. The once cheerful candy-striped wall paper was covered with a plume of blood, brains and slivers of bone.

Danny suddenly felt light-headed and could feel his late breakfast start to rise up. He retraced his steps out of the room and sat with his back to the hallway wall. He took deep breaths to try and keep his Egg McMuffin down where it was supposed to be. He didn't want to be that guy that fouls a murder scene with their own vomit. He'd seen that happen on some of the TV shows he liked to watch. He always thought the people who did were pure dipshit losers.

He put his head between his knees and waited till the dizziness and nausea passed, at which point he knew he would have to call 911.

He didn't notice Craig come up the stairs and approach the room. He was only aware of him when he walked by and stepped into his parents' bedroom.

"Mommy? Daddy?" he whispered.

Danny got to his feet and followed him in. He desperately wanted to grab the boy and take him out of the room but knew he couldn't touch the child.

"Craig, let's go downstairs and wait for the ambulance."

Craig just stared at his parents' bodies. He was just a kid but even at his young age, he knew they were hurt. They were hurt bad.

After Danny went downstairs to call 911, he and Craig stayed in the room till the police arrived. The sun's heat had started focusing on that side of the house. The open window did squat to reduce the temperature in the room. It had to have been well over a hundred. The faint odour had grown into something with a real spin on it. The worst part was that the two bodies kept making sounds from their insides. Danny watched a lot of police dramas and he never remembered once seeing one where the corpses seemed to fart and stuff.

Finally, he heard the sound of multiple cars pulling up outside. Thankfully for Danny, they were the local boys. They knew him and his situation. They understood him when he told them he couldn't touch the boy to move him out of the room and that asking him to come downstairs hadn't worked one single bit. He explained that he'd kinda had to stay with him in the room so as not to let him try to climb on the bed or something.

One of the officers whisked Craig into his arms and carried him downstairs.

Danny felt embarrassed and angry for not having been able to carry out such a basic human action.

Craig hadn't understood what he was seeing in that shabby bedroom. He had at first thought that they had gone to sleep with ketchup on their faces. He was worried when they hadn't reacted to him being in the room and especially when he had called out to them. He'd seen his daddy so fast asleep on the sofa after a heavy night on the jug that his mommy couldn't even wake him. He just assumed that they were both in that condition this time.

The one thing that did give him pause were the flies. There were a lot of them. Mostly buzzing around their heads, but some had actually landed – especially around the darker area of the ketchup. The place where their heads weren't the right shape any more.

Just before the policeman picked him up to take him downstairs, Craig saw a particularly big horsefly land right on his dad's open right eye. He couldn't fathom why he didn't brush it away. It had to itch like the dickens.

A woman arrived just moments after the second police car. She wasn't wearing a uniform but all the police officers and techs seemed to know her. She was very nice to him and even made him his PB&J. It wasn't as good as his mom's but it was close.

After he'd eaten, she asked him a bunch of questions. She seemed most interested about the previous night and his having heard the thunder without seeing any lightning.

More and more people started arriving – some even put on white overalls with hoods. After a while, the nice woman took Craig upstairs to his bedroom where she asked him to show her his favourite clothes and toys. He wasn't sure what *she meant as he really only had one prized possession. Sealy. It was a stuffed toy meant to look like a seal sitting up on its front flippers. Its left eye was gone and some of the fake fur had worn away but Craig loved it as much as he had when it was given to him as a baby. As for his favourite clothes – he only had two pairs of worn jeans, a few T-shirts and one pair of sneakers that fit. The only thing he had that was close to new was a heavy coat he wouldn't get to wear again till the summer heat was replaced with the icy wind that came down from Canada in the winter.*

The nice lady bundled his pathetic belongings into a shopping bag and took him back down the stairs. She spoke to a couple of policemen, then led him out to her car.

As they drove away from the only home Craig had ever known, he had no idea that he would never see it or his parents again. Even though his mommy and daddy had provided questionable stability since they'd taken up their relationship with the jug, they were still his parents. They were the only people he'd ever lived with. They were the only people he'd ever loved, though even Craig knew that that love had changed recently. It had gone from a comfortable, happy feeling that brought daylight into a darkened room whenever he saw them to something darker, something that wasn't anywhere near as comfortable. Craig had started feeling the need to have them reassure him constantly that they still loved him.

Still, they were the only mommy and daddy he'd ever had. He just assumed that all kids felt that way.

CHAPTER
FIVE

Craig glanced back and smiled as he saw that Tim and Sally were both staring out of the SUV in rapt appreciation of the natural beauty that surrounded them.

Living in the high desert at the base of the Vermillion Cliffs offered a lifestyle that few could imagine. The stepped red hills changed colour by the minute. The water was clean. Wildlife was plentiful and varied. The only sounds were those that either you or nature created.

Craig turned off their drive onto the Johnson Canyon Road and then a couple of minutes later turned west onto State Highway 89. Twelve minutes later they were in the town of Kanab, county seat for Kane County in Southern Utah.

Its buildings were as eclectic a mix as was its population. Worn out single-wides sat on tiny lots strewn with broken appliances and car parts that no one would ever use again. Only a few hundred yards away, gleaming custom two-storey homes sat on two-acre lots. Rusted out Studebakers sat one driveway apart from brand new Range Rovers.

The main street was dotted with quaint restaurants sidled right up next to motels that could have been used as the set for Alfred Hitchcock's *Psycho*. Newly built four-storey chain hotels overlooked diesel repair yards.

Despite the funkiness of the place, Craig and his family loved it. There was something indescribably comfortable about Kanab. It felt real and more importantly, it felt safe. There weren't too many places left that you could say that about.

One Saturday a month the whole family went into town. Each adult had their own to-do list. Another great thing about Kanab was that once you were there, shopping was easy as pie.

Craig signalled and turned left into the parking lot of one of the town's two supermarkets. They tried to rotate their business between them to keep it fair. On that day it was to be Honey's that got the honour. Jenny took the kids with her as Craig ran across the street to the town's hardware store. He had a long list of bits and pieces that were needed to maintain the house and the outbuildings. The store usually had everything they needed. On the rare occasion when they didn't carry the specific item, he'd drive into St George – eighty miles away. Craig loved the fact that you could walk into the place and get greeted by name. At a Home Depot you were lucky to find anyone who'd even talk to you.

By the time he got back to the parking lot, Jenny was just emerging from the market.

"Get everything?" he asked.

"Yup. I hope you don't mind but you're cooking ribs tonight. They were on special."

"Fine with me so long as you make that Asian salad with blueberries."

Jenny laughed. "I think you mean dried cranberries and, yes. I bought all the fixings."

"What else do we need?" Craig asked as he helped her unload the piled shopping cart and got the kids back inside and strapped in.

"Can we stop off at Family Dollar? I want to see if they have that hair stuff that smells like Hawaii. Someone besides myself has been using it recently."

"I don't know what you mean." Craig feigned innocence.

"Just so long as the other deputies think you smell pretty," she teased.

"I use a little 'cause it reminds me of you."

"What a load of…"

Craig theatrically cleared his throat and tilted his head towards the kids who were watching their parents from inside the SUV.

"Nice catch," Jenny grinned sheepishly.

The Family Dollar did have the conditioning cream and it was on sale. Jenny bought two. One was for Craig so he could stop having to hide his addiction.

Up until recently, they always stopped at the Three Bears ice-cream parlour, but they'd sold up a while back and their building had been torn down and replaced with a fancy French restaurant. Craig just couldn't fathom why anyone would have thought it a good idea to try to bring French cuisine to a small town like Kanab; then again, their fries with mayonnaise dipping sauce were damn tasty. They'd tried them the one and only time they went there. Their budget didn't allow for too many dinners out. Like a lot of the restaurants that had materialised in Kanab over the past few years, the French place wasn't cheap.

They were sat at what had at first seemed a nice enough table until halfway through the meal when a couple with electric guitars set up and performed not three feet from Craig's right ear. It might not have been so bad had they been halfway good. They were nowhere close to the halfway mark. They were downright awful. That, coupled with a sixty-dollar dinner check, was enough to ensure that the restaurant would have to somehow do without their custom in future.

With no ice-cream parlour any more, their monthly routine called for a quick stop at the Wendy's just before leaving town so they could pick up some of their branded Frosty ice cream to eat back at the house. It had originally been suggested that they should eat it on the drive back, but Craig reminded everyone that he was driving a county car and that chocolate stains on the upholstery would be both unsightly and highly inappropriate.

The drive back took the usual twelve minutes almost to the second. That was another nice thing about living where they did. There were never any real traffic problems. Sure, in the summer when every RV and boat trailer in a thousand-mile radius headed out to Lake Powell, the road got busy, but it never really slowed or clogged.

Once they'd unloaded the Explorer of shopping and children they sat on the back deck and ate their tubs of ice cream. Jenny took twice as long as the others to eat hers probably because she was responsible for trying to ensure that the kids didn't dribble the ice cream onto their clothes. In reality, it was only Tim that needed watching. He reminded Craig of Pig Pen in the *Peanuts* comic strip. You could leave him alone in a sterile room and a minute later he would be filthy. Sally somehow always remained spotless. And was probably the neatest eater of all of them.

"We forgot Steeler!" Sally suddenly exclaimed.

"I thought things were quiet," Craig said as he went inside to open the utility room door.

Moments later the 120-pound Lab came bounding onto the back porch. He was so excited, he didn't know who to greet first. So, in his own goofy way he tried to brush up against everyone at the same time, then rolled on his back which was code for 'urgent belly rubs needed'.

After getting sufficient attention, Steeler spotted a squirrel minding its own business as it scampered across their back wall. The dog couldn't get off the deck fast enough. He managed to knock over two chairs before charging down the wooden steps as he headed for the wall.

Steeler was not a jumper, except on people. Once he reached the wall, he could do little but place his front paws on the adobe bricks and bark up at the squirrel. The squirrel was a regular visitor on their property and knew Steeler's limitations. It twitched its tail a few times then continued on its way.

Craig smiled as he tidied up the ice-cream detritus and headed to the kitchen. As he passed the mirror he realised that he was going to have to get it up on the wall as soon as possible. One head butt or tail swipe from the yellow beast could tip it over and smash it.

He emptied one of the bags from the hardware store and retrieved a picture-hanging kit complete with wire, various sizes of eyelets and a bunch of extra-large picture hooks. He retrieved his hammer and after a short struggle, he managed to open the kit and dump the contents out onto a side table.

With a couple of large eyelets in hand he turned to the mirror and immediately knew that it wasn't a one-man job. The thing was heavy and he needed to get to the back of it.

"Jen?" he called out. "I need an extra pair of hands here."

A moment later she joined him after settling the kids on the couch. Together they pivoted the thing on one corner and turned it so that the mirror part was facing the wall. Jenny watched with growing amusement as Craig tried to screw one of the eyelets into the back of the frame. He couldn't even make a mark, let alone screw it in. Craig ended up using his cordless drill and his smallest bit to at least make a starter hole. Even that was hard work. Eventually he got both eyelets in place and the wire triple-stranded between them to support the weight.

He and Jenny agreed that if the mirror was mounted with the bottom on the floor, it would stick out because of the thick baseboard that ran along the bottom of the living room walls. It was decided that the bottom of the frame would rest on top of the baseboard which could take some of the weight if the wire stretched and also help keep the thing safe from inadvertent bumps from the vacuum.

Craig took a few measurements then hammered the biggest picture hook he could find into the wall. He and

Jenny then had the arduous task of lifting the mirror high enough so Craig could get the hanging wire over the hook.

It took a few tries but the wire finally lay safely in the crook of the hanger. They very slowly allowed the mirror's weight to settle fully onto the hook. Two things happened at the same time. The weight of the mirror pulled the hook off the wall together with a lump of plaster and also bent both eyelets right out of the back of the mirror. Deflated, they lowered it back to the floor.

Jenny could hardly contain her laughter. "Do you suppose that's why there were no holes from previous hangings?" she asked.

Craig was studying the top of the frame. Though Jen had been joking, she'd made a good point. The thing was old. It had to have been hung before – so how?

After going over it a dozen times he saw that buried within the carved filigree were two holes, one on each side of the frame, that showed wear as if something had rubbed within them.

He pointed them out to Jenny.

"The only way this thing's going to stay on the wall is if I screw it to the studs."

"That sounds very permanent," she mentioned.

"It will be. Theoretically, according to Real Estate law it becomes part of the house when it's attached like that," Craig advised.

"We'll worry about that when and if the time comes for us to sell the place."

It took close to an hour to get the mystery mirror securely mounted onto the wall. Exhausted, they stood back and admired their work. At that moment Steeler came loping into the room. He spotted the mirror and approached it with cautious curiosity. He was used to mirrors so he wasn't fooled by his reflection. That didn't stop him from examining it very closely. It obviously held a long history of interesting smells. His final act was to touch his nose to his reflected one. The moment he did so, his tail dropped and swung beneath his legs. Steeler let out a whine like they'd never heard before and crawled backwards on his belly away from the mirror.

Once he felt he'd reached a safe distance he charged out of the room with his tail still between his legs.

"That's a good start," Craig joked.

"Yeah, and not remotely creepy," Jenny added.

CHAPTER
SIX

The next morning, Craig got up well before the rest of the family so he could get an early start. He wanted to get to the office before his shift started and check the few traffic cams on HWY 89 and in Kanab. He was hoping to get a glimpse of the delivery truck that dropped off the mirror.

Sunday was a working day for Craig. He was the only deputy willing to take the Sunday shift. In fact, before he joined the sheriff's department they had never even had a Sunday shift. Kane County in Utah followed the Mormon work protocol. Sunday was a day for temple and family time. The sheriff had to really push the idea of a Sunday shift to the town council. It had taken some persuading, but the idea of having someone on duty when the sunburned and hungover boaters all tried to get home from Lake Powell at once was too good an opportunity to miss.

Craig was one of the very few city or county government workers who was not LDS. He didn't consider himself much of a believer in any organised religion. Jenny had been raised Catholic but had, over time, grown apart from the church and her faith. When they first arrived in Kanab, they had been approached to join the temple but had politely declined.

Despite all the negative press that the Church of the Latter Day Saints received (almost entirely from non-Mormons), Craig and Jenny found them to be warm, decent people. Their children were raised with traditional values that were refreshing compared to those outside the faith.

Craig managed to grab an energy bar and sneak out of the house without waking anyone, including Steeler. Since the hanging of the mirror, he refused to sleep in the living room as was his normal routine. Instead, he was curled up under the kitchen table. Craig made a mental note to try and reintroduce him to the thing when he got home. Steeler was a goofy dog. He'd sidle up to the most vicious-looking dog as if it was nothing, yet something as innocuous as a dragonfly could send him howling back into the house. Maybe they could try hanging a sheet over the mirror and expose a little more of it each day until he felt calmer about it.

The drive in was uneventful but awe-inspiringly beautiful. The sun was rising behind him illuminating just the tops of the red cliffs to the west of Kanab. The openness of the high desert bothered some folks. For Craig, it was probably the most cathartic way to live that he could ever imagine. He had spent a chunk of his youth within the urban sprawl of Phoenix and was happy to never see a city again and not feel that he'd missed a damn thing.

The nice lady introduced herself as Julie Maddow. She was in her late twenties and was taller than she'd ever hoped to be. She watched her calories and kept active to make sure that she didn't add to her volume by putting on any unneeded weight. Her brown eyes were only just visible beneath black bangs that desperately needed cutting. She explained that they had to make one stop before driving to Phoenix.

Craig didn't understand why she would want to take him there. The only time he'd been to Phoenix was when their neighbours had a spare ticket to the circus and took him along. He doubted she was taking him to the circus.

The first stop was at Julie's office at the Mesa Police Department. She sat him in one of the interview rooms, but kept the door open while she made some calls. The people at the station were all very kind to him. He was offered cookies and sodas almost constantly. He declined, however when a woman officer asked if he wanted to watch cartoons on her iPad, he couldn't refuse.

He was giggling at an old episode of Sponge Bob Square Pants when Julie stuck her head around the corner.

"You ready to go?" she asked.

"Can we go home now? Mommy and Daddy might be all better now."

Julie tried not to show the emotion she felt at hearing those words. She knew that the little boy's life was about to go over the cliff. She had already spoken to the Phoenix branch of the ADCS (Arizona Department of Child Safety) and they had authorised his stay at an emergency child shelter.

Julie was tasked with tracing family relatives in the hope that there would be one that was both suitable and interested *in adopting the boy. If that didn't pan out he would end up 'in the system' either in a foster centre or if he was lucky, in a foster home until he was adopted. Even that was far from guaranteed. Because of the circumstances of how he'd become orphaned, many people would shy away from the child as if he could still be carrying some hereditary artefact of their death.*

The Brightstar emergency shelter was in a suburb of Phoenix that had seen better times. It had once been considered a funky-chic part of town for young artists who had gotten bored with the finicky nature of the upscale clients in Scottsdale, but hadn't yet earned their chops to show in Sedona. They nested within the shabby older brick buildings while honing their crafts. Art exhibits took place only a few doors away from flop houses and soup kitchens.

Eventually, the artists, sick of the crime and filth, moved on and the chic feel magically evaporated. Funky then devolved into blight and the neighbourhood fell into a decrepit state of unattended lethargy.

The staff must have been waiting for Craig's arrival as a man and a woman appeared at the door before Julie's car had even come to a full stop. What Craig didn't know was that Julie couldn't even think of leaving her car unattended in that part of Phoenix. Where once elements had been brought together to create art – now things were stolen to be broken down and sold as parts.

Craig sat in the car as the adults talked for a few minutes. Occasionally one or both of the shelter staffers looked over at him and smiled.

Julie opened the car door and unstrapped Craig from his car seat. She introduced him to the pair then retrieved his menial possessions from the back seat and handed them over.

"These nice people are going to look after you now. They will make sure you have plenty of food and toys and that you are kept safe," Julie said.

She had wanted to add 'love' to the list of things that would be provided but knew full well that that was the one item that he was unlikely to get for a while. Once you were in the system, you became a number, not a person. Few people realised how many children get handed over to places like the ADCS sponsored shelter.

Divorce, suicide, drugs, alcohol, abuse, paedophilia, depression – all could result in a young child ending up without their parents. It was an epidemic. The national numbers were staggering. Julie just hoped that Craig had the stuff that was needed to survive with his sanity intact.

The sheriff's station where Craig worked was located in the centre of Kanab. It was wedged between the state liquor store and an auto parts supply shop. Neither was open, nor would they be on a Sunday.

He unlocked the single deadbolt and turned on the overhead strip lights. The outer office where he sat was utilitarian. There were no frills, no luxuries and no attempt to make the place look like anything other than a functional police station.

Craig dumped his things at his desk then went back to the tiny utility kitchen. It was basically a mini fridge, a sink, an electric kettle and a microwave. There was no coffee-maker of any kind. Coffee, like alcohol, was forbidden in the Mormon faith. In order to satisfy his caffeine habit and not offend his co-workers by taking up space on the counter with a coffee-maker, he'd given up fresh brewed in favour of instant. He kept his jar of Nescafé at the far back of the cabinet behind a jar of peanut butter that didn't look as if it had been touched in years.

With a mug of instant coffee in his hand, he sat at his desk and switched on the computer. When it finally booted up, he logged into the Kane County website. He then had to log in to a separate link to access the county sheriff's site.

He checked his email on his .gov desktop then, finding nothing urgent, followed another link to the Kane County highway camera portal. In a county where people don't lock their doors there was very little need for security video so he had to settle for the two traffic cameras in Kanab (there were only two traffic lights) and the few along HWY 89 heading towards Page, plus the one in Fredonia just across the border in Arizona on HWY 89A.

Thanks to the jerk who chose to wake up the whole house, Craig knew exactly what time the delivery truck had been at his property. He first checked the camera fifteen miles east of their turn-off on HWY 89 coming from Page. Between midnight and 6 am the highway cameras automatically switched to motion sensing. There just wasn't enough night-time traffic to waste data recording space.

Craig clicked through the short video hits starting at thirty minutes before the unwelcome door knocking had begun.

The first vehicle recorded made Craig smile. It was Jake Willis – another deputy. He would have gone off shift in the Big Water area just outside Page and was returning home to Kanab.

The next one was an older model RV heading west as well. There wasn't another hit for ten minutes. He played that clip but the screen was black. Once outside the town, the highways were unlit so without illumination provided by each car, there wasn't much to see but usually there was at least a trace of some sort of light until the vehicle passed out of the camera's capture arc. Craig stared at the screen and noticed something pretty weird. Some object did move across the black screen. It was as if a shadow that was darker than the black screen had been recorded by the roadside camera. Craig made a note of the time and continued watching the remaining hits. Having had no joy finding the truck prior to the delivery time he went through the same search routine for any vehicles after the truck had left the property.

There were only four hits in the hour following it leaving his house. One of them was again of a black screen. Craig could have sworn he saw the same shadow as before but going in the other direction.

He made a note of that one as well. He planned to send them to their IT specialist up in Salt Lake City. Maybe she could tell him what was wrong with the camera or the recording.

He checked the Kanab and the Fredonia camera feeds but none of them had captured an image of the delivery truck anywhere close to that time of the morning. It didn't make any sense. He had checked the only routes that the driver could have taken.

He then lowered his head in a gesture of self-chastisement. There was another route. He'd never known a delivery truck use it but the driver could have bypassed Kanab entirely and turned off HWY 89 in Glendale, thirty miles to the north and driven down Glendale Bench Road till it became Johnson Canyon Road. It was narrow, curvy and a pain to drive but theoretically, it could have come that way. If it had, there was no way of tracking it. There were no cameras in Glendale or anywhere north on 89 till you got to Panguitch and that was almost seventy miles away. It would be impossible to tell that truck from any other.

Disappointed, he reopened his desktop and checked on any incidents that may have occurred on Saturday that needed follow-up.

CHAPTER
SEVEN

Craig got home just after 5 pm and was met at the car by Jenny.

"You need to do something with your dog," she advised. "He's acting wackier than usual. He's been staring across the room at that damn mirror almost since you left. He won't go anywhere near it. He just sits at the other side of the sofa and stares. Oh, yeah, and he growls!"

"Growls? No way. He's only growled once in his life and that was when that guy put his hand on you at the gas station."

"I remember. The poor man had to have been eighty. He just wanted help working the pump," Jenny smiled.

"Let's go have a look at this fierce animal." He put his arm around her waist as they walked into the house.

Sure enough, Steeler was crouched down at the far end of the living room glaring back at the mirror. Craig approached him and rubbed the back of his head. He looked up at Craig with his big brown eyes and let out a quiet whine followed by a sigh.

"What's the matter, big fella? It's just bits of wood with some glass in the middle," Craig explained. "Come and have a good sniff."

He took hold of Steeler's collar and tried to coax him over to the other side of the room. The dog was having none of it. He froze in his swatting position and let out a heartfelt cry.

"Don't force him if he doesn't want to get near it," Jenny insisted.

"I know if he'd just have a really good sniff he'd be fine," Craig replied.

"Well, don't make him cry. Let him do it in his own time."

Craig released the collar and rubbed one of Steeler's ears (Steeler's favourite thing ever). The Lab again looked up into his eyes, only this time, Craig could have sworn he saw a mix of fear and sadness in them.

"I'm not hinting or anything but the ribs have been marinating since this morning and the Asian salad with cranberries is ready and waiting," Jenny smiled.

"I guess I'd better get the barbeque going," he replied, rolling his eyes as if it was some sort of great burden.

The fact was he loved it when he had an excuse to fire up the old Webber instead of the propane barbeque. He believed that certain meats needed the smoke from mesquite and charcoal to really bring out the flavour. He considered himself to be an expert charcoal lighter. He started by laying a deep bed of briquets onto the metal rack insert in the centre of the Webber's concave base. He then used an electric starter element. He didn't approve of using any of the chemical or petroleum-based fire starters. He swore you could always taste a slight trace of them in the finished product.

Thirty minutes later the coals were covered with a thin veneer of white ash. Craig announced the barbeque to be ready for action.

They sat outside under a pair of heat lamps and ate at the wooden picnic-style table and benches that Craig had built himself. He'd even modified one bench to have a fold-up back section so a booster seat could be attached.

Jenny had covered the table with a plastic red and white chequered cover. There was no messing around when it came to ribs and children. They had the innate skill to be able to spread BBQ sauce in ways that defied the laws of physics. Each person (adults and children) had their own monogrammed (with a magic marker) plastic bib. Two rolls of paper towelling were positioned in the centre of the table.

Craig raised his bottle of O'Doul's amber non-alcoholic beer.

"To the mountains, to the fields, to the heavens and to family." Craig pointed the bottle to the red hills behind them, to the high desert scrub lands below, to the sky and to Jenny, Tim and Sally.

They repeated the toast with their beverages. Tim hadn't been able to wait and had pre-emptively attacked one rib. He already looked like some sort of flesh-eating monster. He had sauce covering his face from his nose to his chin and had even managed to get some on his neck. He was beyond the cleaning capacity of mere paper towelling, and that was just from the first rib. By the time he was finished, if precedent was anything to go by, he would look like something that needed a high-power pressure wash. Craig had offered once to put him through the mini car wash in town, but Jenny hadn't found that suggestion to be the least bit amusing. Probably because she wasn't one hundred per cent sure that he was kidding.

The fact was, neither was he.

Craig smiled contentedly as he took a swig of his fake beer. He'd actually grown to quite like the stuff. It didn't give you a buzz but, it was the buzz that he was trying to avoid.

Craig didn't adapt well to life in the shelter. He couldn't understand why they wouldn't let him go home. The ADCS had tried to help by providing a child psychologist to gently discuss the death of his parents and what all that meant. The hardest part was having to explain to him that he wouldn't be seeing them anymore. The staff had suggested that maybe by having Craig attend their funeral, it would help him start the mental transition. The psychologist had strongly advised against that. He felt that it would be much too distressing for the young boy, especially as he really wouldn't understand what was going on.

As it happened, there was no funeral as such. There was no one to arrange anything so formal. His parents had no family that could be traced and no friends. At least none that wanted anything to do with their funeral. There was also no visible indication of either parent having been remotely religious. They had died owing money on the house and had even taken out loans encumbering their old car.

With no estate, no wills and no money, they were given a pauper's service and were cremated. Their ashes were kept in a zip-lock bag within a sealed cardboard box at the crematorium. It went into their back storage area in case someone ever came forward to claim their remains.

Craig began having nightmares, then a few days later he began two months of sporadic bed wetting. The shelter decided that the psychologist needed to come back and give the poor boy a few more sessions. It never dawned on them that the nightmares had started after the initial session and that perhaps the pro bono shrink may not have been the best option for the boy.

Nobody at the shelter could remember how Dr Adams had been approved by the ADCS to minister to the psychological needs of young children. All they could recall was that one day he arrived with all the appropriate paperwork confirming his licencing, state accreditation and contract with the ADCS. He had been the designated child psychologist for the sanctuary for three months prior to Craig's arrival.

There hadn't really been time to tell if his treatments were helping as he explained that in most cases there could be a six-month or longer period of regression when the patient would actually seem worse as their psyche started to repair itself.

During Craig's third session alone with Dr Adams, the shelter manager forgot they were in the tiny conference room and having unlocked the door, inadvertently barged in to retrieve a fresh notepad from the stationary cupboard.

The sight that greeted her would ironically end up sending her to therapy for many years.

Craig was lying naked as a jay bird on the conference table as Adams held a video camera above him. The child's eyes were red as if he'd been crying. The psychologist's eyes were wide with shock over being discovered. For one crazy moment, he thought of trying to deflect the situation with anger at being interrupted during a confidential clinical session. He chose instead to try and make a break for it by shoving the young manager out of the way then making for the front door. He knew that if he could get out into the sprawl of the city, he could disappear as he'd done many times and in many cities in the past.

It might have worked had the manager not been an ex-Marine with two tours under her belt. As he reached out to push her aside she grabbed his wrist, twisted it, then pushed down. Adams found himself flat on his back with a heavy boot at his throat.

It turned out that the state-approved psychologist had never even finished high school. He was a known paedophile who had forged professional documents in a number of different states and had been welcomed by the ADCS to spend time with young children.

Once Adams had been forcibly removed by the Phoenix police and two members of the FBI (Adams had driven one young child across state lines), officers tried to ask Craig some questions, but he was practically catatonic.

The manager had the good sense to call Julie at the Mesa Police Department who dropped everything to drive into the city. She was horrified by what had happened. She was given the manager's office so she could spend some time with Craig.

It was slow-going. Craig was happy that the nice lady had come back for him but couldn't overlook the fact that she was the one who not only took him from his home, but had left him at the shelter. It wasn't until Julie started to cry that Craig's defences came down. It was hard to tell who cried the most that afternoon.

While emotions were being released in the manager's office, the director of the ADCS along with a few of his sycophantic flunkies, arrived at the shelter. Brendon Knute was a short man with a big chip on his shoulder and an attitude to match. The director was in his fifties but still tried to dress young. His slicked-back hair and five-button Men's Warehouse suit made him look more like an east-coast gangster than the head of a government agency that assisted vulnerable children.

An emergency meeting was held in the dining hall as the conference room was still full of police technicians who were gathering evidence.

Despite Adams having shown all the supposedly correct documentation when contracted by the ADCS, and it having been that same agency that authorised him to evaluate and treat children in their shelters, Knute decided that the emergency shelter had to close effective immediately. The children currently in the shelter would be distributed out to other facilities or to Phoenix's city foster centre.

When Julie heard what they had planned for the children, she approached the director and did something she had never done in her time as a state child liaison officer assigned to the Mesa Police Department. She asked if Craig could stay with her for a couple of nights while the appropriate housing was found for him.

The director denied her request on the spot. She asked for a moment of his time in private. They ducked into an empty office where she asked that he reconsider, considering the unusual circumstances. With unabashed bureaucratic arrogance, he told her that she needed to mind her own business and stay out of his. He started to walk away.

"Sir, if I may?" She spoke in her 'don't fuck with me' tone. "A child under the care of a facility that was licensed and authorised by your department, was sexually abused. I fully expect that we will find that others within the facility have almost certainly suffered the same fate."

"I had nothing to do with the hiring of that phony," the director pontificated. "The manager of the shelter was responsible for vetting anyone who came into contact with the children. I suggest you focus your blame where it's warranted."

Julie removed a folder from her faux leather satchel. She found the document she was looking for and held it out for the director to see.

"What is this?" he asked.

"I'm surprised you don't recognise it. It's the ADCS authorisation form for Dr Adams to provide unpaid volunteer services to this shelter. It was signed by you just over five months ago. The gist of the wording is that the ADCS has investigated and approved all licensing, educational and background checks of the individual noted above. That would be Dr Felix Adams. What this proves is that you are completely responsible for the vetting and approval of a known paedophile and permitted him to volunteer in foster shelters where he would spend time alone with children without supervision. You have left me *no choice but to file a formal complaint with the governor's office. I very much doubt whether you will be in your position very much longer and as for the ADCS – well, I suppose…"*

"Look, there must be something you and I can do. I mean we don't want harm to come to any of the children," Knute suggested with false sincerity.

"That ship has clearly sailed," Julie fired back.

"Perhaps if I reconsidered your earlier request. Would that make a difference?" Knute offered.

"It might."

"Then, please accept my apology, and of course you may foster the child for a few days while we find other accommodation."

"That's very generous of you but I must mention that I don't fully understand why you are closing this perfectly good, and desperately needed shelter because of a mistake made by you, or at least by your office. The boy most certainly won't be coming back here. Neither will any other victims we may find, but from what I've seen, the staff is excellent and should be given the opportunity of continuing to serve this great city."

The director's face had turned a dark crimson. It was clear that he had never been dealt with in that way and was furious. He also knew that she had him over a barrel.

"I'll give that some thought," he mumbled.

"You do that. That will give me time to write a few drafts of my letter to the governor."

He glared at her with pure hatred.

"The shelter will remain open, but I will be keeping my eyes on it."

"And I will be keeping mine on you." She gave him a fake smile as she walked out of the room. The manager and two staff members gave her a round of applause. They had obviously been standing outside the door listening to the whole thing.

She let them believe that she wasn't going to file a complaint against the director just because she'd got what she wanted. The fact was she'd already notified her supervisor the moment she'd been shown the authorisation document signed by the director.

After cleaning up after the rib dinner and getting the kids to bed, Jenny and Craig watched an old episode of *Justified* on Prime Video. They'd seen the whole series before but Craig loved the show so they were taking a second pass at it. After the first time when they'd binge-watched all of the seasons, Craig came home one day with a brand new beige cowboy hat as was worn by Tim Olyphant, the star of the series. Jenny laughed while wagging her finger.

"Not going to happen, sweetie. It might work on TV but you'll get laughed out of town if you try to make that *your thing.*"

He had been momentarily disappointed but ultimately saw her point. Especially when he wore the hat at one of the sheriff station's spring barbeques and was greeted with snickers and one 'howdy, partner'. The hat rarely made another appearance.

Steeler was still wary of the mirror but got up enough nerve to jump up on the sofa and snuggle up next to Jenny. When the episode was finished Jenny and Craig made their way up to bed. Steeler was usually not permitted to sleep upstairs as the big guy was basically a bed hog who snored so loudly that he used to wake Sally when she was a baby. As they were about to leave the living room Steeler gave them the most pathetic look imaginable from the sofa.

"Oh, all right, ya big wuss!" Craig relented. "Come on."

Steeler could hardly get his feet under him fast enough. He charged off the sofa, gave the mirror a wide berth then dashed past the pair and ran up the stairs.

"Yeah. Like he's the wuss." Jenny rolled her eyes as she followed the dog up.

Craig and Jenny did their usual check on the kids before retiring. They were both sound asleep. By the time they got back to their bedroom, Steeler had already claimed the centre of the bed. He was stretched out on his back with his legs in the air.

He was snoring.

Craig sat up with a jolt. A noise had awakened him. An old house with two kids and a clumsy dog was filled with odd noises throughout the day and night. As a parent you unconsciously learned to filter out all those potential sources.

The sound that woke him was something different. Something new. It was a scratching sound coming from above him. It had to be something in the attic. The strange thing was that the noise seemed to be occurring in different areas simultaneously.

He made a mental note to check up there in the morning. He tried to fall back asleep but for some reason felt anxious. He almost never felt that way since getting over his meltdown all those years ago, but as he lay awake in the dark, he felt another emotion creep up on him.

Craig tried to look impassively at the anxiety and find its origin. Try as he might, he could find no obvious cause for the irrational feelings.

It didn't help when a few minutes later, Steeler began thrashing in his sleep while whining loudly. Jenny laid a hand gently on his belly. The whines eventually turned to submissive whimpers as his legs stopped their flailing. His snoring took over.

"That's better," Jenny murmured.

The next morning, Craig walked into the kitchen and kissed each family member. Even after his quick shower, he was still feeling groggy from lack of sleep.

"Thanks for the surprise." Jenny gave him an extra kiss.

"What surprise?" Craig replied.

"And I thought you hated the thing," Jenny added.

"I'm serious, I have no idea what you're talking about."

"Don't joke like that. You're freaking me out," Jenny said as she studied his face. She could see that he wasn't joking. She grabbed his hand and led him to the living room. She stopped in front of the mirror.

"You're telling me you didn't do this?" she asked.

"Do what?" Craig couldn't see what she was so upset about.

"Look at the mirror. Remember what it looked like when we first unpacked it?"

Craig looked carefully at it but it took a few moments until he finally saw what Jenny was seeing. When they had first unpacked it, the mirror had looked yellow with age. It had also been pitted and had a crack across the top right corner.

The mirror now looked brand new. There wasn't a trace of the age or of the crack.

"Okay. Now I'm a little freaked out as well," Craig whispered so the kids didn't hear him in the other room.

"As far as I know, mirrors don't come with a self-restoration option," Jenny said flatly. "Did you manage to locate that delivery truck?"

"No. There was some glitchy footage that I'm going to send up to Salt Lake today, but other than that, not a trace. I even wondered if the driver had come the whole way along Johnson Canyon Road."

"Why would anyone do that? Especially in the middle of the night."

"Maybe we should take it down," Craig suggested. "We could do it as soon as I get home."

"What'd be the point? It looks even better now."

"I thought you were freaked out?"

"I was," Jenny replied. "I'm not any more. I mean, come on. The only thing that's out of whack here is us. Obviously what we saw was dust and crap from the packing. The crack was probably a splinter from the wood or something. This isn't Hogwarts. We don't have a mirror with special powers."

"That does make more sense. But then, why is it so clean this morning?"

"I ran a Swifter over it before breakfast. That's when I noticed the difference," Jenny advised.

"Mystery solved." Craig nodded his head. "I'm relieved. A self-restoring mirror and creepy sounds from the attic would be a little too much first thing in the morning." Craig checked his watch. "Speaking of which, I'm gonna be late."

"At least have some cereal," Jenny said. "What creepy noises from the attic?"

"I'll check it out when I get home. Probably a squirrel got in and is making a home for the winter."

"I hope it's just a squirrel," Jenny added as they headed back to the kitchen. "The Parsons heard noises last winter and found a whole family of racoons living above them."

Craig smiled and stared again at the mirror. He wasn't as convinced as he pretended. Jenny's Swifter theory sounded pretty good at first, but the more he thought back to when they'd stripped back the brown wrapping paper and revealed the contents, the better he could remember the mirror's poor condition.

As he drove along HWY 89 heading into Kanab, he still couldn't get the mirror out of his head. He could clearly recall not just the yellowing and the crack, but also the edge of the mirror where the backing had worn away, leaving brown marks where the reflective foil had once been. He'd seen his share of cheap old mirrors in that first foster centre in Phoenix. As far as he knew – a quick wipe with a duster couldn't fix something like that.

Once the hospital released him into her care, Julie drove Craig to her town house in North Scottsdale. They'd had to stop at Mesa United Medical Centre so that Craig could have an examination of his private areas as well as having those same areas brushed to save any evidence, such as pubic hair that might have been left by the phony shrink.

The good news had been that the hospital couldn't find any sign of physical abuse during his examination. The forensic team together with the detectives had reviewed the video from the camera. It appeared that whatever Adams had planned for that session had not yet occurred when he was interrupted. That was all well and good, however the boy had still been forced to lie naked in front of an adult tasked with his care.

The psychological damage from that alone could be devastating. She knew that she first needed to get Craig talking, but only when he was ready. She had to find a way to renew his trust in a grown-up before he was likely to feel inclined to share the details of what had happened that day and also what may have occurred during the other sessions as well.

Julie had never fostered a child and despite all her years of working with vulnerable children, she had no idea how to treat one in the confines of her home. Because of her career and the horrific and graphic images of abused children that were burned into her memory, she had lost any urge to have any of her own.

She knew that it was a paranoid reaction, but deep down she felt that she could never guarantee with one hundred per cent certainty, that a child for which she was responsible wouldn't at some point suffer the soul-destroying damage that she witnessed on a daily basis.

Her home was almost monastic. Her life was spent outside of her townhouse. By the time she came through her front door at night, she wanted nothing more than to shower, eat and sleep. She knew hers wasn't a healthy existence, but the children had to come first.

Julie was thankful that she'd stocked up the fridge at the weekend so she could at least offer Craig something fresh and home cooked. She didn't consider herself much of a chef but having checked out the kitchen in his house in Apache Junction, it was obvious that the quality and healthiness of the food that his parents had provided could hardly have been considered nutritious. She'd never seen so much Rice-a-Roni and Kraft Mac and Cheese. She had nothing against either. In fact, she had a box of M & C hidden in the back of a cupboard just for emergencies.

The first thing she did when they got to her house was show Craig her guest room with its small en-suite bathroom. She used the space primarily as her office, but it had a rarely used queen-sized sofa bed. Craig had never seen one before and was mesmerised as she unfolded it into an already-made bed.

"Just like a transformer, huh?" she suggested.

The blank stare she got back said it all. Julie realised that a five-year-old was unlikely to have any idea about transformers yet. She retrieved Craig's stuffed seal and laid it on top of the pillow. Without a word, Craig climbed up onto the bed, gently picked up Sealy then curled up into a ball with his security 'friend' in the middle.

"I'm going to start dinner. Is there anything special you like?"

He didn't acknowledge her at all.

"I'll be downstairs. You can come down whenever you want or just call out if you need anything."

She left him in his foetal position. She made a quick pasta with leftover chicken, fresh basil and cherry tomatoes. She also saved some of the cooked pasta without sauce in case he wanted a different topping.

She checked on Craig regularly but he didn't seem to have moved since he first lay down. At one point, he was so still, she had to watch his chest rise and fall just to be sure he was still breathing.

After dinner, Julie turned on the TV and streamed an episode of The Durrells *on Netflix. She loved the series about a British family in the 1930s that moved to Corfu without any clue as to how to live or survive on the Greek island.*

She had been debating having her nightly glass of wine but was worried that she might need a clear head in case there was an emergency with Craig. She finally decided that after the day she'd had, the only chance of any sleep was if she softened the memories of the events with her one permitted glass of Chardonnay.

It had clearly been exactly what she needed. She fell asleep halfway through the episode. She woke up almost an hour later to find Craig snuggled up next to her on the sofa. He was sound asleep with his right thumb firmly buried in his mouth and Sealy clutched in his other hand. She was glad he couldn't see the tears flowing down her cheeks.

She gently lifted him into her arms and carried him upstairs. She was about to settle him into her guest-room bed, but decided that he obviously needed the comfort of another human being. So as not to disturb him, she passed on her pre-bed bathroom regime and just lay there, fully clothed, next to the small child.

They both slept through the night.

CHAPTER
EIGHT

The first thing Craig did when he got to work was email the dark video hits from the highway camera to Salt Lake City. He could have sent it on Sunday but even though he wasn't LDS, he wanted to show his understanding of the 'no Sunday' work ethic and not be seen to be sending correspondence on that day.

Kane County was hardly rife with major crime. Things like rape and murder were almost unheard of. There were some suicides, burglaries, drug offences and domestic disputes but mostly, it was traffic offences that seemed to fill their report sheets.

Kanab was a small town built on an S-bend on HWY 89. Tourists and truckers seemed to feel that the speed limits were there as suggestions rather than legal maximums. The town was almost equidistant between Zion, Bryce and the Grand Canyon national parks. Between early spring and late fall, the highway was busy. The visitors were excited and distracted, the truckers, exhausted and also distracted.

Sometimes that could lead to some truly horrific accidents.

That Monday was no exception. At a few minutes before eleven, the first call came in. There had been an accident between an eighteen-wheeler and a RV just south of Glendale about thirty miles north of Kanab.

Craig and Gary Clarkson, the other deputy on duty, drove separately and reached the accident thirty minutes later. A local volunteer peacekeeper had cordoned off the accident area and was funnelling traffic along one lane so HWY 89 didn't seize up entirely.

The vehicles had been travelling in opposite directions on a section of highway that had a designated third-lane passing zone. The middle lane was the pass lane only when one side of the lane showed yellow dashes instead of solid lines. The driver with the dashes on their left was permitted to pass if the road was clear and conditions were suitable.

It was very apparent that the driver of the motorhome had either not known the rules or had ignored them. The RV appeared to have been coming around the corner as the semi was passing a laden tractor and trailer. The motorhome chose the same moment to try to pass a slower vehicle, but did so by crossing the solid yellow line.

They had collided head on with the eighteen-wheeler. The truck's front end was badly dented but looked entirely fixable. The thirty-six-foot RV however, was unrecognisable for what it was. It had concertinaed into only a quarter of its length then exploded as one of its propane tanks ruptured. Whether it was the impact or the explosion, Craig couldn't tell at first glance, but what was left of the RV had disintegrated as it tumbled a hundred feet down the adjacent hillside.

He and Gary could count five bodies from where they stood on the edge of the road looking down. Three of them were children. There was no need for closer inspection to check if they were alive. None of the bodies was fully intact.

The driver of the big-rig was sitting on the bottom rung of his cab's running board. Someone had put a blanket over his shoulder and given him a plastic bottle of water. He was talking on a cell phone. He looked to be in shock and had clearly been crying.

Craig and Gary were joined by a 'go team' from the NTSB (National Transportation Safety Board). They rarely investigated road accidents, but with the truck having been a commercial vehicle on an interstate highway plus the death of an entire family, it put the crash right in the middle of their wheelhouse.

Police officers and sheriff deputies arrived from as far away as St George and Cedar City. Volunteer fire personnel came from every fire house in a hundred-mile radius to help collect the remains of the shattered RV as well as to assist the recovery of the bodies at the bottom of the ravine.

They were there until after dark. A gentle snow began falling soon after sunset, making the climb up and down the ravine too treacherous for work to continue.

Thankfully, by that time, there wasn't actually that much more to be done. The semi had been towed away to a storage shed in Glendale and the scattered parts of the RV were trucked to Kanab as each crane-load was retrieved from the hillside.

The five deceased members of the Peterson family had been brought up the hill one at a time in mountain rescue sleds. All work ceased as each body was laid onto the roadside. In almost complete silence, everyone watched as each family member was loaded into a waiting ambulance and was taken to the mortuary at the Kane County Hospital in Kanab. Even though they were in individual black body bags, it was very obvious which ones contained the children. They in no way filled out the one-size-fits-all bags. There was also less strain on those carrying them. They were lighter as well as smaller.

As the ambulances drove away, Craig noticed an elderly Native American man staring at him from the other side of the yellow police tape. Craig was distracted for a moment by the crane's engine going silent. When he looked back, the man was gone.

Craig left the scene at 7 pm. He thought of taking the shortcut that he suspected the delivery truck might have used, but decided that with the darkness and an increasing snowfall he wasn't going to risk it. Five deaths in one day was more than enough.

As he neared Kanab his cell phone rang. He picked it up and was shocked to hear Jenny yelling at him. It was completely his fault. They had a tradition that every day he went to work he would call her as soon as he got there to say he was safe. He'd forgotten completely that morning and had then spent the day in an area with no cell reception. To make matters worse, when she started to get worried, she called the sheriff's office only to get a recorded message as everyone from the office had been ordered on site at the accident location.

She calmed down slightly after he explained what had happened but he could tell that she was still pissed off at him for having not thought to get in touch with her through some means. He knew that there was only one thing he could do to warrant full forgiveness.

He stopped at Honey's Market in Kanab and headed straight for the bakery section. He grabbed a full-size coconut and salted caramel sponge cake. It was her favourite and saved for very special occasions only. To go one step further in the attempt to bring her around, he also bought a tub of their favourite cashew-milk salted caramel and chocolate ice cream. It wasn't that anyone had any leanings towards veganism, they just adored the taste. They tried to keep consumption of that cake and ice-cream combo to a minimum as they feared that if they didn't maintain that policy they would end up binge-eating it every night. It was that good.

As he walked in the door, he handed her the cake and ice cream before she could even speak. She looked down at the bag then back up at him. She was about to say something when Sally came running into the room.

"Is that Honey's cake?" she stuttered as she jumped up and down with excitement. "I knew Mommy was mad so I hoped really hard that you'd go to Honey's."

Jenny rolled her eyes knowing that Craig had pretty much got out of the jam. As she was making room in the fridge to store the cake until after dinner, she lowered her voice so Sally couldn't hear. "There's a funny noise coming from inside the walls now."

Craig walked around the house and held a water glass against the walls while holding his ear against it. It wasn't exactly state of the art but it still amplified sound. He couldn't hear anything unusual.

He promised to do a full attic to basement check the following morning as he desperately wanted to relax and try to get the images of the crash site out of his head, but Jenny was concerned about everyone losing more sleep because of the attic noises.

They reached a compromise whereby he would have a quick check in the attic right then, and do the bigger survey on Saturday. Being an old house, access to the attic was a chore. There was only one ceiling hatch and it was located in the bathroom. There was no pull-string and no dropdown steps. The only way to get up was with a ladder. The hatch was only two feet square. Because of the bathroom layout, there was no room for the full leg spread of their folding ladder. Craig also had to finagle getting the thing up the stairs and into the small room. It was impossible to get a safe angle for climbing so he had to brace the bottom of the ladder against the bath, then with Jenny holding it steady, climb up almost vertically. It was not a task for the faint of heart.

Craig reached the hatch, slid the bolt lock open (a concession to Tim when he'd become convinced that there were monsters everywhere in the house, including in the attic) and pushed the square wooden insert upwards. Of course, it resisted. Craig didn't have enough distance to apply good leverage so he basically punched the thing. Thankfully it came loose and vanished up into the darkness above.

He moved further up the ladder until he could squeeze the top half of his body through the opening. He reached up into the blackness and felt for the vertical stud on which was mounted a truly scary looking on/off switch from what Craig guessed was the 1930s.

He felt around and finally found the switch and flipped it on. The bulb was only a 75W incandescent, but it was plenty bright enough for him to be able to see most of the space. The centre of the attic looked like it always did. Dusty and empty. They didn't store anything up there because of the physical limitations of what would fit through the hatch and to say nothing of the problems of trying to get anything up the ladder.

The edges of the attic where the angled roof met the floor were in complete darkness. Craig realised that he should have brought up a flashlight but he'd assumed that the overhead would be sufficient. He was about to ask Jenny to get one when he saw something out of the corner of his eye. Something in the dark recesses moved. It was impossible to see what it was but Craig knew he'd seen something darker than the shadows move even further from the light.

"Jen, can you grab my Maglite from the bedside table?"

"I can't do that and hold the ladder," she advised.

"I'll do it, Daddy," Sally volunteered.

She ran down the hallway and was back in seconds with his mini-Mag. Jen climbed a couple of steps so she could get it into his hand.

Craig turned the metal focus head and the light came on, flickered then settled to a pale yellow. He'd forgotten that the batteries were almost dead.

He decided to make do. He swept the dim light over to the dark areas where the hanging bulb couldn't reach. It took him a moment to comprehend what it was that he was seeing. His feeble light wasn't piercing the darkness enough for him to clearly make out what was there but it was enough to illuminate their eyes. They were everywhere.

Craig must have accidently squeezed the handle of the Maglite because the strobe feature activated. The pale yellow light began flashing every half second.

The critters didn't like that at all. They began to move into the spread of the overhead light. For some reason it reminded Craig of an old sepia movie.

He was able to recognise the interlopers as mice, squirrels, chipmunks and even racoons. He fanned the strobing light around the attic dark spaces and saw animals everywhere. They then began to approach him. They didn't look healthy. Their eyes had a yellow tinge and were coated with a mucus-like film, though the yellow part could have come from the Maglite's failing batteries. Craig somehow didn't think that was the issue. A few of the racoons seemed to have foamy drool at the corner of their snarling muzzles.

Craig desperately clawed for the hatch insert. The animals were getting closer. He couldn't find it. He knew the board could only be a matter of inches away from his hand. He stretched a little further and finally felt the wooden edge. He started to lower himself out of the opening so he could drop it in place. He knew he had to step down lower on the ladder to accomplish that manoeuvre but his brain had gone into lockdown mode.

He managed to get his feet moving but lost his footing and slid down three rungs before he got control. He somehow got the hatch into its square housing before losing his footing again and sliding down the rest of the way. Jenny and Sally were staring at him as if he'd gone crazy.

He was about to explain when he noticed he hadn't bolted the hatch closed. He scampered up the ladder and slid the lock home.

"What the hell's wrong with you? You could have broken your neck!" Jenny scolded.

"Mommy said a bad word. Mommy said a bad word." Sally danced off down the hall repeating the refrain.

"I think we need to call pest control," Craig said as he tried to get his breathing back under control.

"There won't be anyone who'll come out in the dark. I'll call Bugsy's tomorrow. He's the best in town and I'm sure will sort out the problem."

"Tell him to bring an extra big truck," Craig quipped.

"What exactly did you see up there?" Jenny asked.

"Forget it. It was just the perfect end to a really crappy day."

"Well, I've made spaghetti Bolognese from scratch so that should cheer you up," she offered.

"Let's not forget the cake."

"I thought that the cake was a present for me. Now you expect to have some as well?" she scorned jokingly. "Go get cleaned up. The spaghetti will be ready in about fifteen minutes."

The meal was delicious. It was one of Craig's favourites. Somehow Jenny managed to make it taste better than he'd had anywhere – even at restaurants.

They followed it up with the salted caramel cake and a scoop of the salted caramel ice cream. It was beyond decadent.

They retired to the living room and watched *Frozen II* for the umpteenth time. They made it a point to always watch child-friendly programming while the kids were awake. They saved the good stuff for when the kids were both tucked up in their beds, sound asleep.

Sally had developed a strange obsession with the first *Frozen* movie then developed another one for the sequel. She had to see it at least a couple of times a week or she would have a super tantrum. Craig watched it with her (again) and was surprised that despite all the previous dozen or so viewings, he still quite enjoyed it. Possibly more than Sally who, despite the pleading to watch it again, got bored halfway through and joined Tim on the floor playing with a Lego castle kit.

Craig finally started to feel more relaxed. He had managed to compartmentalise the horrors of the crash and the subsequent animal zombie epidemic in the attic, and was finally enjoying the calm of a family evening together.

Then the doorbell rang.

"Who the heck could that be?" Craig asked.

"Only one way to find out," Jenny suggested.

Craig reluctantly got up off the faux leather sectional and headed to the front door. He opened it and was shocked to see the old man he'd seen staring at him at the accident site. Up close, Craig could see that the man wasn't just old, he was ancient. His dark wrinkled skin looked heavily weathered by many years of high desert living. His green eyes showed no sign of age and seemed wise as well as piercing. His long raven-black hair showed no grey and Craig doubted that the guy was into hair dye. A single turquoise clip bunched it together at shoulder height.

"Can I help you?" Craig didn't even try to hide the sharp edge to his voice.

"The question is whether I am in time to help you," the visitor replied.

"I don't know what you're selling but we're not buying," Craig responded bluntly. "Please don't come to our house again."

Craig started to close the door.

"Have you taken delivery of the portal yet? It probably looks like a mirror."

Craig reopened the door.

"Who are you? What do you want?"

"My Hopi name is Ahote and I am here to hopefully save your lives."

CHAPTER
NINE

Julie left Craig sleeping in her bed. He hadn't stirred once during the night. She was making oatmeal in the kitchen when she heard the sound of padded footsteps approaching. Craig was still wearing the same clothes as yesterday though he had donned a pair of worn bunny rabbit slippers. He still looked sleepy.

"Hi. How are you?" Julie asked.

He just stared down at his feet.

"Would you like some breakfast?"

His head nodded once. It was almost imperceptible. Julie opened her pantry door and showed him the cereal shelf. She wasn't proud of it but she was something of a cold cereal junkie. Not for breakfast oddly enough, as she felt that that meal needed to be healthy. But on countless nights when she would come home exhausted and often distressed, she found a bowl of sugary cereal to be strangely cathartic. She assumed it was something to do with her own disjointed childhood. More often than not, cold cereal had been the only constant in her life.

"Do you want to tell me which one you like?"

Craig shuffled over to the pantry door and looked at the shelf loaded with an amazing array of brightly coloured cereal boxes. It reminded Julie of one of those articles about food health. Her shelf would be pictured in the 'what not to eat' section.

Craig pointed to a box of Kellogg's Frosted Flakes. She took it off the shelf and showed him the front of the box.

"You're sure?"

He nodded.

"You go sit at the dining table and I'll get you a bowl and some cold milk," Julie said.

Craig ended up having two bowls of the sugary flakes, all the while staring fixatedly at the picture of Tony the Tiger on the box.

After Julie cleared up the breakfast things and waited for her old-fashioned upright coffee-maker to finish percolating, she knelt down in front of Craig.

"Would you like a bath?"

He shrugged his shoulders.

"I think it would be a good idea. You could put on clean clothes afterwards. Wouldn't that be nice?"

She was delighted when he looked up to meet her gaze and nodded. It wasn't unusual at all for victimised children to prefer to remain in their dirty clothes. Their soiled condition was sometimes the only consistent thing they knew and they could be highly reluctant to alter that condition. Psychologists referred to it as 'the dirty diaper syndrome'.

Julie ran a bath as Craig looked on. She checked with him a number of times to make sure the water was at the right temperature for him and that the amount of water in the tub was at a level he was comfortable with.

When it came time for him to undress, she left the room to give him his privacy.

"If you need anything, just call out. Okay?" she said as she partially closed the bathroom door.

She intended to wait in the hall until she heard him safely settle in the bathtub.

She was caught off guard when Craig opened the door and stepped back into the hallway.

The faded Elmo T-shirt was stuck half on – half off. Julie had noticed it seemed too small for him, but didn't want to say anything.

"Help, please," he whispered while wiggling his right arm which was stuck vertically up in the air.

Julie put a hand across her mouth to stifle a laugh.

"How did you ever do that?"

"Don't know," he replied shyly.

"You look pretty silly, you know?" she smiled at him. "Look in the mirror."

He stepped back into the bathroom and examined himself in the full-length mirror. He looked up at Julie and suddenly started to giggle.

"I do look silly."

She gently pulled an arm free of the shirt and lifted it over his head.

"Is that better?" she asked.

He nodded.

"Mommy helps me wash," he stated.

"Would you like me to help you?"

He nodded.

Once Craig was bathed and dressed in clean clothes he sat next to Julie on the sofa and watched his morning cartoons. Julie decided to try her luck at asking him a few questions while he was calm and mildly distracted.

She asked about the fake psychologist and was relieved when Craig told her that he hadn't touched him at all. She studied his face closely to make sure he wasn't just scared to tell the truth. She asked him about being naked and he replied that the doctor told him he had to take his clothes off before he could talk to him and that all the children had to undress first. He said it was the rule.

She could see that he wasn't particularly upset by the experience so she decided that it was best for Craig to not make an issue of the matter.

Julie was about to call her office to say she was running a few minutes late and would be bringing a friend to work when she was interrupted by her doorbell.

She opened her front door and recognised the two police officers from the Mesa division. She gave them a warm smile.

"Jim, Nate, what can I do for you?" she asked. "Do you want to come in for a coffee?"

Nate was the bigger of the two and had been friends with Julie since high school. He looked uncomfortable.

"Jules, we're here because of a formal complaint that was made by the director of the ADCS."

"What sort of complaint?" she asked, her voice tensing.

"It's pretty serious, Jules," Nate replied.

"That's complete BS and you know it. I filed a complaint about him yesterday so he's just trying to

do the same thing back to me. What did he say I did? Threaten him? In that case – okay, maybe I did, but only with an internal investigation. There's hardly the need to send you guys out."

"Actually," Nate continued, "his complaint was that you removed a vulnerable child from one of their shelters and proceeded to take him back to your home where he spent the night."

"That's exactly true. The shelter called me after an incident at their facility. The child couldn't remain there so I brought him home with me. I will be making longer term arrangements for him today."

"According to the complaint, you have no authority to remove any child from an ADCS facility without their prior consent. In addition, you are not registered as a licenced foster-care provider with either the county or the state."

"Oh, come on. You both know me. Anything I ever do is solely for the good of the child," Julie insisted. "The guy is lying. He gave me permission himself. That a-hole director is just trying to get back at me. I really can't believe anyone bought his story."

"I agree with you, Jules, but the problem is that a warrant was issued for your arrest," Nate stated.

"On what charge?" she gasped.

"I'm afraid it's charges. Child endangerment and unlawful removal of a minor from a foster facility."

Julie's jaw dropped open. She was so stunned that when the other officer removed his handcuffs and approached her, she thought for a moment that she was being pranked.

Craig chose that moment to poke his head around the corner.

"Well, hi there, big fella," Nate said. "How are you today?"

"She let me sleep in her bed and gave me a bath, too!" he replied cheerily.

Both officers turned to face her. There was no longer any sign of friendship whatsoever.

CHAPTER
TEN

Craig stared at the old man with growing anger. He was about to give him a piece of his mind when he noticed that Jenny and the kids were standing in the hall watching the whole thing.

"Would you like to come in, Mr Ahote?" Jenny offered.

Craig gave her an 'are you out of your mind?' glare.

"It's just Ahote, Mrs Edmonds. It's Hopi for 'restless one'. I thank you for the invitation but I won't enter your home at this time." Ahote turned to Craig. "Perhaps we could speak outside for a minute?"

Craig knew he had no choice at that point but to accept as Jenny was now monitoring their exchange. She always saw the good in people. Craig, having spent years as a sniper then as an officer of the law, had trouble seeing the good in anyone. He grabbed his winter coat and a wool hat and stepped outside. He led the other man away from the house. He had no intention of letting Jenny hear what he had to say to the man.

"What the hell do you think you're doing coming to my house saying that you're here to save our lives?"

"My actual words were that I hopefully could save your lives," Ahote replied. "There is a force that has entered your home. It intends to steal the lifeblood from a member of your family."

"Was that gibberish supposed to be some sort of a clarification? I've never heard such bullshit in my life. Stealing lifeblood!? What the hell does that even mean? You can't just turn up at a house and threaten a family. You do know that I am a deputy sheriff, right?"

"I am aware of that, yes. You must understand that I am here only to help you. I won't, nor would I ever, threaten you in any way. This force that has entered your home comes just before the arrival of Beyath as she transitions from the fifth realm."

"That's enough. I want you off my property right this minute. If you refuse to leave I will have no choice but to arrest you," Craig stated as he turned to walk back to the house.

"Have the creatures of the night begun nesting in your attic yet?" Ahote asked.

Craig froze. "How did you know that?" he asked.

"They always come before Beyath. The force that precedes her arrival attracts the wild ones. They sense her power and wait to serve her, though sadly that same force drives them insane."

"Look, Ahote. I am an agnostic from way back. I don't believe in religions, gods, the supernatural or some woman who attracts vermin. Yes, I have some pests in my attic, but that's because it's winter. We always get some critters that find a way inside where it's warm and they can nest. I don't know what you really want or what you're selling but we're gonna pass. Okay. So please leave us alone."

Craig started to turn away from Ahote then had a thought.

"Why were you at that accident earlier today?"

"That's another precursor to the arrival of Beyath. The death of entire families often occurs just before she transitions to the first world and takes human form."

Craig gave him an incredulous look. "Again, thank you for stopping by but I've got to ask you for the last time to leave – now."

"When you wish to talk to me again, I will be at the end of Old Mesa Road. You know it?"

"Of course, I know it. I also know it's been closed for over ten years."

"Just remember. I'm at the very end of the road."

"You certainly are at the end of the road," Craig said shaking his head in disgust.

Craig watched as the man climbed into a very tired-looking Jeep Cherokee and start to drive away. Ahote stopped the Jeep and manually wound down his window.

"You may want to look into your wife's family history. Check out disappearances every twenty-five years."

Craig glared at him without a word. Ahote shrugged and wound up his window. Craig didn't take his eyes off the old Jeep until it had reached Johnson Canyon Road and turned left towards HWY 89.

"So, what did he want?" Jenny asked, the moment he walked back in the house.

"You wouldn't believe it if I told you." He rolled his eyes.

"Try me."

Craig looked around for the kids.

"They're in bed. You can tell me in the kitchen while I finish clearing up," Jenny advised.

"Crap. It was my turn."

"You've had a bad day. I can cope with a few plates."

They settled at the dining table. Craig cast a not particularly subtle glance at the remains of the cake that was still out on the counter.

"Just a small slice," Jenny said. "I don't want you turning into one those men I see at the St George Costco. I'm warning you now. The day you come home with stretchy pants and a gut, I'm outa here."

"Ditto," he shot back.

Jenny laughed as she placed two slices of cake onto the dining table. Craig gave her a cagey smile.

"So, what did the old guy want?" she asked as she brushed crumbs off her mouth.

"It was all a little strange. I think the poor man was actually a little screwy," Craig stated.

"Screwy how?"

"He had some cockamamie idea about some old woman who was going to return to this realm and restore her human form."

"Okay. That certainly qualifies as screwy. What's it got to do with us?" she asked.

"That's the weirdest part. He was convinced that her…

I think he called it transition… had already started and that she was coming here through a portal."

Jenny ate another mouthful of cake as she pondered what he had just said.

"Why here? What have we got to do with an old lady and a portal? Do we even own a portal?" she asked.

"It appears we do," Craig replied with a smile. "It's the mirror. Supposedly the mirror is the portal," he mumbled through a mouthful of cake.

"Well, that explains everything," she replied sarcastically.

"He even knew about the critters in the attic," Craig added. "He said that they're attracted by the force and congregate where they can best serve her."

"Boy, that guy really was off his meds."

"I told him to basically fuck off and leave us alone. As he was driving away he had one more gem to add to the whole encounter."

"I can hardly wait." Jenny shook her head.

"You're going to love this," Craig said. "He said that we needed to look back at your family tree. He said to look for family members who disappeared at twenty-five-year intervals."

"That's creepy," Jenny stated.

"I know. What a jerk. Huh?"

"No, I mean that's creepy because one of my aunts did disappear."

"You never told me that."

"Every family has dark stuff. I just never thought to tell you about her," Jenny explained.

"That's awful. Were you guys close?" Craig asked.

"Not at all. I only ever met her once. She lived in the UK. There was a huge family reunion over there. I think I remember hearing that she disappeared shortly after that."

"I doubt that was what the old man was talking about."

"Why do you say that?" Jenny asked.

"She was too far away – I think. When exactly did she vanish?"

"God, I don't remember. I was just a kid."

A huge gust of wind whipped around the exterior of the old house causing it to creak and wail.

"Wait, I know," she exclaimed. "The entry stamp going into the UK is in my old passport."

She dashed out of the room leaving Craig alone with an unfinished cake sitting only a few feet away. He was about to give in to the craving and reach over to the counter when Jenny came back into the room with the passport in her hand.

"That's weird."

"No stamp?" he asked.

"No, there's a stamp. January 29, 1996."

They stared at each other, then spoke at the same time.

"That's twenty-five years ago."

Another blast of wind hit the house. It was strong enough to make it groan.

Then the lights went out.

CHAPTER
ELEVEN

Julie was handcuffed and placed in the back of the police patrol car. The officers stayed on the front stoop with Craig as they waited for something.

After ten minutes, a late-model burgundy Cadillac DeVille pulled up next to the cruiser. Brendon Knute slowly stepped out of the car so the two policemen would have time to be impressed by his wheels. They took one look at him in his shiny suit and Cadillac and both thought the same thing.

Pimp. They were surprised when he introduced himself and showed them his ID. He advised them that he was to take charge of the young boy. They had been expecting an ADCS staffer, but if the director chose to turn up in person, that was fine by them.

The moment Julie saw Knute pull up, she started shouting from the back seat of the police car. Nate finally broke away and slid into the front seat.

"Jules. For God's sake, calm down. I don't want to have to make things worse for you by adding resisting arrest."

"You don't understand," she cried. "That's the asshole I complained about. He's the one that filed the report on me."

"That may be, but my orders are to hand the child over to an ADCS representative," Nate explained. "He's the director of the ADCS. I have to let him take the boy."

Julie was about to argue when Knute knocked on the police car's window. Nate opened the car door.

"Perhaps if I could have a word with Ms Maddow, I could explain that everything is being done to ensure the care and safety of the boy," Knute suggested.

"If you think it would calm her down, then go ahead. Why don't you sit in the passenger seat and I'll leave you both alone?" Nate suggested.

Knute slid into the front of the patrol car as Nate got out.

"I'm sure you weren't expecting to see me so soon," he purred as he smiled at her through the plastic partition.

"You are a piece of shit. Why are you doing this? It's not just me you're hurting. What about the poor boy?" Julie shouted.

"That's very easy to answer. Your attempt to extort me – which by the way, you completely failed to do, gave me few options. Had you bothered to do a little research beyond finding one document you thought you could use against me, you would have learned that the mayor of Phoenix happens to be my brother-in-law. So, here's what's going to happen. You are going to lose your job and never be permitted to work with children ever again. I know that seems harsh but that's what happens when you threaten me. As for the boy, *as you've taken such a keen interest in his situation, I of course must now do the same."*

Julie sat silently glaring at him. A single tear ran down her cheek.

"I will be driving him to the Maricopa Centre for Children with Special Needs where he will almost certainly remain until he is old enough to be let loose on society. It's a shame. A nice-looking boy like that would have probably been adopted quite quickly, but with his violent temper and the biting issue – little details I added to his file, I doubt anyone will want to bring him into their home."

"You bastard. Why would you do that to a child?"

"Because, my dear Ms Maddow, I know how much pain it will cause you. For the rest of your life you will know that your little threat at Brightstar has destined the poor boy to a childhood of misery and loneliness. I personally don't know how you will ever manage to live with yourself."

"Why not at least let him go back to the Brightstar shelter? That's a thousand times better than the Mariposa Centre," she pleaded.

"You didn't actually think I was going to keep that place open, did you?" Knute smiled as he checked his hair in the visor mirror. "I couldn't in all fairness to the children let such a mismanaged facility continue to exist. The staff have all been given their notice. They, like you, will also never be able to work with children again."

"You are a monster," Julie whispered menacingly.

"And you are a cunt, Ms Maddow."

He gave her a warm smile as he opened the cruiser door and advised the officers that she was feeling much calmer.

As Julie was being driven away, she looked back and saw Knute holding Craig's hand. Craig seemed to be trying to free himself but the director was smiling as he waved goodbye.

Julie prayed that Knute wouldn't really destroy the childhood of a small boy just because of her actions the previous day.

The fact was the director meant every word that he had said except about taking him to the Mariposa Centre. He had no intention of sending him anywhere where she could find him.

The first thing that Knute did was to have Craig's name changed by emergency decree after he convinced a judge that the boy was in danger. He produced two letters, purportedly from the fake psychologist, in which the paedophile threatened Craig's life. He blamed the boy for his being discovered and would not rest until he found him and dealt with him.

The judge immediately agreed to the name change and Craig Winchell became Craig Edmonds. Knute then made arrangements for him to be sent to the city of Flagstaff in the northern part of the state. Craig was to live at a large and very poorly run foster home. It housed over thirty boys ranging in age from six to sixteen. At five, Craig would be the youngest. The Red Rock Foster Centre was one of the ADCS's dirty little secrets. It was where the unadoptable children were sent.

Located three miles outside of Flagstaff, it was remote, wild and very private. The kids housed in the camp-style bunkhouses were clothed with donations that even the large charities didn't want. Their food was starch driven and flavourless but it kept them alive.

The staff consisted of one middle-aged couple who managed the place, three staff that doubled as teachers, though none had any accreditation whatsoever and a cook who was also the handyman and groundskeeper. There was no cleaning or laundry service. That function was performed unwillingly by the children.

The facility received close to $300,000 a year from the state to care for the children. Only a quarter of that ever reached them. The rest went into a number of different pockets with Brendon Knute receiving the largest share of the 'stipend'.

The Red Rock Foster Centre had no website and was not listed anywhere as an adoption facility. In the twenty-year history of the place, not one boy had ever left the centre except by ambulance, pine box or expulsion at the age of sixteen.

This was where Craig Edmonds (née Winchell) was supposed to spend the next eleven years of his life.

Life, however, is what happens when you are making other plans (or so the saying goes). In Craig's case, events did indeed alter Knute's best-laid plans. His time at Red Rock was cut short by ten years and four months.

The forestry service annually carried out a series of controlled burns around the densely forested hills that encircled Flagstaff. An unexpected windstorm took control of one blaze and sent it on a path to a remote wooded area east of the city. That put it on a direct heading straight for the Red Rock Foster Centre.

Red Rock had no evacuation plan and no way to transport the children out of harm's way. To make matters worse the husband and wife managers drove off in the facility's minivan leaving everyone else to fend for themselves the moment they heard that the fire was heading their way. Thankfully, the Flagstaff Fire Department knew of the foster centre and could see that they were in the path of the fast-moving blaze.

They commandeered a school bus and with a water truck as escort, evacuated everyone from the facility. The children were housed in a school gym in Flagstaff where other fire evacuees were being taken. Volunteers were shocked at the state of the boys. Their clothes were torn and filthy. They looked half-starved and many were showing early signs of malnutrition. They fed and clothed the children and provided books and toys to keep them occupied. They tried not to notice that the older boys seemed to be only able to read at a fourth-grade level.

Because of Craig's young age, he became the centre of attention. Peter Sable – a local reporter in Flagstaff, heard about the young boy and felt that there might be a good human interest story in there somewhere.

He visited the gymnasium and was equally shocked at the condition of the children. He interviewed the older kids and the only staff member who had stayed with them once they were rescued. He started to piece together the appalling truth about the Red Rock Foster Centre. The story was turning into something else entirely. In newsroom vernacular – it had legs. It didn't take Peter long to trace partial ownership of the facility back to the director of the ADCS in Phoenix.

He decided that instead of bullishly charging ahead and confronting the man, he wanted to get some serious background for the story. He already had the villain for the article. What he needed was the star victim. The one with which everyone would sympathise.

Craig fitted that role perfectly.

Peter's story could have hit a number of bureaucratic brick walls which would have made it very hard to research the article. But Brendon Knute himself, though unaware of the fact, made it possible for Peter to cut through to the juicy part with surprising ease. The thing was that while Knute was the power behind the Phoenix branch of the ADCS and had some connections in the mayor's office, he was universally despised by his co-workers and peers. Grasping at the opportunity to dethrone the tyrant, they decided to lift back the carpet and let the public see what filth had been hidden beneath.

Peter's little human interest puff piece ended up being Phoenix's Watergate. The tendrils of mismanagement and corruption that spread out from Brendon Knute, ultimately ravaged City Hall, the entire Arizona foster system and most importantly, the case against Julie and the subsequent vengeful treatment of Craig.

Julie was released from the minimum security women's penal facility outside Tucson. She had been awaiting her trial and was denied bail as she was considered a flight risk thanks to a convincing letter from the mayor's office.

A settlement was reached even before she returned to her town house. Being both an intelligent and a careful person, she had no intention of spending any of the $450,000 that she cleared after lawyers and taxes. The interest would serve her perfectly well. The bigger victory was getting her job back and having her tarnished reputation redacted entirely.

Julie never considered herself to be a particularly vengeful person, but when she was asked whether she would consider appearing for the prosecution when Brendon Knute eventually appeared before the bench, she was only too happy to accept.

The happiest moment was when the district of Mariposa County granted her the accreditation to be able to foster children. There was only one child she wanted to help. The young boy who had inadvertently started a ball rolling that ended up knocking local government pins in every direction.

Craig wasn't aware of any of the goings-on down south in Phoenix. A local Flagstaff family had agreed to temporarily foster him after the evacuation. The husband and wife were in close touch with Julie and knew that she was working hard to get final approval to foster Craig. They all agreed not to say anything, just in case things went off the rails.

Finally, they heard the news they'd been hoping for.

When the doorbell rang, they told Craig that he should answer it.

He opened the door and looked up at Julie's teary face. Though in reality he hardly knew her, she had shown him more love in the short time they'd spent together than he'd received in years. Without a word, he stepped into her arms and began to cry.

CHAPTER
TWELVE

"Go into the living room," Craig ordered. "The fire's still going and you'll be able to see in there. Meanwhile, I'll go check out the fuses."

Jenny made for the living room as Craig grabbed his heaviest coat and stepped out into the frigid darkness. He walked to the side of the house and felt along the wall till he found the metal flip-front box that housed the old-fashioned fuse panel. He made a mental note to repaint it some other colour than yellow. Jenny had done that so that it didn't stand out. Now he understood why it needed to do just that.

He lifted the front and felt along the bottom of the unit. He pushed aside some cobwebs then found the mini LED flashlight he'd left there for just such an occasion. He turned it on and pointed it into the box.

He felt a wave of panic and dizziness.

The box was filled with what looked like white cotton candy. Dotted everywhere were yellowish sacks suspended in the wispy material. In a few places he could see movement.

He knew exactly what he was looking at. It was a black widow spider's nest. He guessed there were at least two dozen egg sacks and couldn't be sure how many had hatched.

Craig hated spiders.

The fact that he'd had his hand in there feeling around for the flashlight made him feel nauseous. He suddenly took the flashlight in his other hand and shone it on the back of the one he'd had in the fuse box. His hand was clear. He was about to shine the light back into the box when he noticed a thin strand of something on the cuff of his winter coat. He turned his arm and saw that the strand was actually a spider's leg feeling its way along the heavy material of the jacket.

He turned his arm a fraction more and saw the black widow in its entirety. It was a big one and it was making its way slowly up Craig's arm.

He cautiously but quickly unzipped the coat and slipped out of it. He laid it on the gravel intending to stomp on the interloper. He shone the light onto it and saw that there was more than just the one. There were at least a dozen of the black arachnids. Most were still on the sleeve but a few had made it as far as the shoulder.

Craig shivered and began swiping at his arms, shoulders and back.

After what an onlooker would have assumed was an attack of St Vitus' Dance, he decided that he was spider-free and ran to the workshop. He found his old winter work coat behind the door as well as his work gloves. He grabbed a can of engine starter fluid and a box of extra-long matches he kept for lighting campfires, a long two-pronged metal stick that was usually used for marshmallow roasting and one of his automotive-sized fire extinguishers.

Fully armed, he headed back to the fuse box.

He shone the light back down onto his coat and couldn't see any of the spiders. That didn't actually make him feel any better. In fact, it freaked him out even more. He preferred knowing where they were.

He lit one of the matches and held it in front of the fuse box. He flipped off the cap on the starter spray and depressed the nozzle so that the spray went above the flame. The result was impressive. The improvised flamethrower sent a horizontal plume of fire into the infested box. Craig stopped and checked the results. The webbing was blackened and shredded. The sacs were on fire. As he watched, one popped open and dozens of baby spiders exploded out of it.

"Screw that."

He gave it another burst of flame. He checked again. On the bottom of the box one very large spider was writhing in agony. It was obviously the mother. Its body was almost completely charred yet it was still trying to move and protect its brood. Craig watched until it had stopped moving altogether then sent a blast of foam to extinguish the few tiny flames that were still going.

He stood well back as he used the marshmallow prong to clear away the remains of the spider massacre. He was finally able to see the old rectangular ceramic fuses. He removed the master fuse and saw that the heavy gauge wire had burned and split in between the prongs that held it in place.

Pre-cut lengths of different gauge fuse wire were in a small metal tin at the back of the box along with a mini screwdriver. Though not relishing the task, Craig had to remove the gloves to replace the broken fuse wire. He had one last check around the inside of the box but saw no sign of any survivors.

He replaced the wire then eased the ceramic block back in the fuse board.

The outside lights came on. Craig was then able to see what damage he'd done to the fuse box. He was glad to see that other than a little charring here and there, everything had survived. He doubted that would have been the case with a modern plastic set of breaker switches.

He closed the box and looked down at his winter coat strewn onto the gravel. He wanted to retrieve it but just couldn't bring himself to pick it up quite yet. Maybe in the morning.

Proud of his accomplishments, he headed back to the front of the house. He was just about to open the door when he heard Jenny scream.

Craig charged into the house calling out her name.

"I'm in the living room," she shouted.

He found her sitting on the edge of the coffee table. She looked shaken and scared. Steeler was sitting next to her trying to look protective but he looked almost as scared as Jenny.

"Are you all right?" Craig asked as he visually checked her over. "Are you hurt?"

She looked up at him and forced a weak smile.

"I'm fine. I may have just creeped myself out. When the lights were still off, I went upstairs to check on the kids. They were both fast asleep. As I walked back into the living room, I looked at the mirror for some reason."

"That would be because you're a woman," Craig jibed.

Jenny ignored the comment.

"When I looked at it… I couldn't see my reflection. For a fraction of a second, I felt I was looking at another room. It wasn't ours. Then the lights suddenly came on and I just screamed. I have no idea why."

"Sounds to me that you screamed because you looked into the haunted mirror," Craig replied with a straight face. "Is it possible that what you actually saw was our room but that the firelight was causing weird shadows that made it look different?"

"What about not seeing my reflection?" she asked.

"Maybe you looked at the mirror before you were fully in front of it. If you looked at it from an angle, you wouldn't have seen yourself."

Jenny thought about what he'd suggested.

"It probably makes more sense than what I just said," she admitted. "I don't know why that thing gives me the creeps. It's so beautiful."

"Maybe it's just making us think it's beautiful so that the ghost can pass through it when its ready," Craig said in a corny Dracula voice.

"We have a ghost?" Tim asked excitedly from the hallway. Sally was standing next to him and clearly didn't share in Tim's excitement.

"Mommy. I don't want us to have a ghost," she whimpered.

"Maybe it's in the attic," Tim further suggested.

"Nooo!" Sally exclaimed as her eyes started to widen.

Jenny went over to her and took a knee so she was at eye level with her daughter.

"We don't have a ghost. Your daddy was just teasing me."

Sally looked over at Craig with as much of a scowl as a four-year-old can muster. "That's mean, Daddy!"

"I'm sorry, pretty girl. I won't do it again," Craig replied sincerely.

"You better not!" Sally added.

"Come on, you lot," Jenny said, "let's get you both back to bed."

As Jenny wrangled the kids back upstairs, Craig took a moment to study the mirror. He couldn't see anything unusual about it. He carefully touched the centre of it, not really knowing why. It was solid just like it was supposed to be. He took his finger away but not before unintentionally leaving a greasy soot mark on the glass.

Unaware, Craig turned away and headed for the couch.

Behind him, the dirty mark left on the mirror shimmered for a second then disappeared completely.

When Jenny returned, they curled up on the couch and created an account on *urhistorynow.com*. Jenny plugged in the details of her family going back three generations. Craig was amazed. He knew who his birth parents were but hadn't a clue about previous generations. Jenny knew names, dates and even general locations for everyone.

When the data had been loaded and the fee paid, a family tree began to populate before their eyes. It started with the newest information then worked backwards. By the time it reached the 1930s it had slowed down but was still filling in the squares.

The 'time remaining' bar had started at ten minutes but by then was showing seven hours plus. They decided to go to bed and let the software do its thing overnight.

They checked on the kids then went to their room and snuggled under their extra heavy winter quilt. They were asleep within minutes.

Craig had his first dream of the night shortly after that.

He was back at the accident site outside Glendale on HWY 89. He was watching the body bags being lifted onto the road side. When all five were lying in a row, the first ambulance arrived. Before they could load the first one, Craig thought he saw movement within the heavy black plastic. He stopped everyone from doing what they were doing then carefully unzipped it.

A stream of scrawny and sick-looking squirrels, rats, mice, racoons and even foxes staggered out of the opening. He could tell that they were all rabid. He warned everyone to back away.

One of the workers called over that another bag was moving. Craig stepped over to it but didn't want to open it. Then he heard a small child's voice.

"Help me. I'm scared."

Craig was almost too stunned to react. People were shouting at him to open it. He finally knelt next to it and unzipped it. As he spread the plastic apart, he saw a very young girl with the left side of her face entirely missing. Her one eye stared up at him as her half mouth pleaded.

"Please help me. They hurt."

"What hurts?" Craig asked.

"The spiders."

Craig was about to ask *what spiders?* when the first one crept out of her open head wound. It was a black widow but much bigger than any he'd ever seen. A second one was close behind. Soon there were dozens. As Craig backed away, the girl became buried beneath a writhing mass of black spiders. They soon filled the body bag and began to overflow onto the highway macadam.

Craig woke up screaming.

Jenny sat up and took his hand.

"You had a dream. It was only a dream. You're here now and you're safe."

Craig looked to her with relief and let out a huge sigh. Jenny suddenly looked terrified.

Craig tried to say something but couldn't seem to talk. His mouth felt full of something and it was moving. He looked down and saw that a stream of black widows was moving down his chest. He suddenly understood that they were coming out of his mouth. He tried to scream but at that moment they all began to bite.

He woke up screaming. The first thing he did was shove two fingers into his mouth and check for spiders.

"What are you doing?" Jenny asked.

"I had a mouthful of spiders." He realised as he said the words that he sounded pretty lame.

"I must have been dreaming," he mumbled.

"I would think so. Come here." She eased his head into her lap and ran her fingers through his damp hair. "You haven't had the bad dreams for a while," she said soothingly.

"I know. This wasn't anything to do with Iraq. This was different."

"If you have PTSD, it's all related. Do you want your meds?"

Craig thought for a moment. "No. I think I'd better stay clear-headed."

"Then let's try and get some sleep, okay?" Jenny gently suggested as she kissed him on the cheek.

Craig rolled over onto his back. "Sorry, babe."

"You never have to apologise to me."

Craig closed his eyes and soon fell asleep again. He dreamed a lot that night. None was as graphic or as realistic as the first one, but they were all pretty bad.

He finally got out of bed at around 5 am. He couldn't sleep and didn't want to wake up Jenny with all his squirming as he tried to find a comfortable position.

He made himself a cup of camomile tea then went into the living room to see if the ancestry site had finished its search. The site had automatically logged them off, but Craig saw that they had an email from them. It advised that the search was complete and provided a link to their dashboard. Craig felt a little guilty about seeing Jen's family tree without her being there, but she wasn't likely to have time to see it anyway until long after he'd left for work.

He was about to open the DISPLAY TREE tab when Steeler slunk by the mirror then ran into the room. As soon as he saw Craig he started his morning sideways-wiggle dance that was half pure excitement, half 'where's my breakfast?'. Craig followed the Lab into the utility room and put a scoop of dry food into his bowl. It was a big scoop for a big dog. He buried his face in the bowl and with happy snaffling sounds, finished it in less than thirty seconds.

Steeler then sat back on his haunches and looked up at Craig with sad, begging eyes.

"Don't give me that pathetic 'I'm so mistreated' look," Craig whispered. "Is it all the beatings that you get? Is it the lack of attention?"

The big eyes stayed locked on Craig.

"You are such a goofball!"

Craig opened the side door and let him out for his morning property inspection and toiletries. Craig headed back to the living room to have a quick look at Jenny's family tree.

As he walked past the mirror, he sensed something odd. He couldn't see himself and thought he had seen a different room reflected in his peripheral vision. He turned to face it and saw only a reflection of himself and the living room. It was just as Jenny had said had happened to her the previous day.

He realised that he had fallen for the same trick of light. He hadn't turned on the lamps so the living room's reflection could look pretty strange. There was something else, but he couldn't quite bring the thought to the surface. He shook his head and plopped down on the couch next to the laptop.

He refreshed the page then clicked on the TREE tab. He was stunned at what opened. Jenny's tree started in 1827 and had two distinct branches. One in the US and one in the UK. Craig didn't care about indirect descendances. He was only interested in close relatives specific to her.

He needed to take three screen shots to capture the whole thing. He emailed it to himself so he could do some research later.

"What ya doing?" Jenny asked, scaring the hell out of him.

"How do you come down stairs and make no noise?" he asked. "That is so creepy."

"I come from a long line of creepers," she smiled.

"I know. I've just been looking at the list."

"You didn't wait for me?" She sounded disappointed.

"You never have time in the morning. I just had a quick peek."

"Let me see." She stepped towards him.

Craig patted the space next to him on the sofa. Jenny studied the tree and like her husband, was stunned at how far back her family history was documented.

"Okay, so here's Aunt Gina in the UK branch. We know she disappeared in 1996," she said as she pointed at the screen. "Let's see who else we have…"

She ran her finger over each branch until she suddenly stopped at one entry.

"I heard about this guy – Andrew Reed. He was my great uncle. I only know about him because he disgraced the whole family way back when."

"Disgraced how?" Craig asked.

"He was engaged to some society girl and the day before the wedding, he ran off. No one ever heard from him again."

"That sounds suspiciously like a disappearance, doesn't it? Any idea of the date?"

"That shouldn't be hard to find," Jenny replied. "As I said, it was a major scandal."

She opened Google and entered his name and the word *wedding*.

Sure enough, the page populated with a bunch of newspaper articles about the daughter of Wyoming state senator, Arnold Westfield, being basically left at the altar. The senator made no bones about the fact that when he found the scoundrel, he planned on strangling him with his bare hands.

"What's the date?"

Jenny felt her world tip just a fraction when she read the date at the top of the scanned copy of the *Wyoming Herald*. January 27, 1971.

"That's twenty-five years before Aunt Gina," Craig stated.

Before Jenny could reply, Sally appeared in the hallway rubbing the tiredness from her eyes.

"Mommy, I'm hungry," Sally said in a very sleepy voice.

"I guess I'll have to look at this later."

"See what I mean?" Craig joked.

CHAPTER
THIRTEEN

Julie had no real idea how to raise a child though she certainly knew what not to do. She'd witnessed that first-hand on far too many occasions. What made it work was that Craig had hardly come from what could be called a nurturing environment himself, so between the two of them, they managed to put the puzzle together, piece by piece, day by day.

Despite his neglected early years and the horrific event that took away his birth parents, Craig grew into a very normal and happy child followed closely by becoming a sombre and moody teen. Thankfully, he grew out of that phase as soon as his interests moved from darkly destructive interstellar warfare games to girls.

The transition was almost instantaneous. One morning, her sulking adopted son slunk off to school as usual but then returned home with story after story about this new girl that had just started in his class. He was smitten.

The game console began to gather dust as Craig's infatuation ebbed from one girl then transferred to another. He started dressing with more care. Solid black clothing was replaced with apparel that had actual colour.

Julie was unspeakably relieved that the happy Craig had returned. He remained that way through his teens, right up until the jetliners crashed into the Twin Towers, the Pentagon and the field in Pennsylvania.

Craig seemed to take the attack personally. He'd never been remotely patriotic or even that interested in current affairs but the moment those towers collapsed, something inside him changed. He suddenly felt the need to serve his country and avenge those who had died on 9/11.

He obtained Julie's signature on his enlistment form as he was still only seventeen, then reported to the Marine Recruit Training Depot in San Diego. For the next thirteen weeks he was transformed from an unskilled Arizona teenager into an American fighting machine.

He arrived at Camp Pendleton in Southern California to continue his training, determine his strongest skillset and begin the process of specialisation. By the time he turned eighteen, Craig had become an amazing marksman. He'd never even seen a gun up close (except the one lying on the bed between his mommy and daddy) yet he could hit a moving target at a thousand yards. Every time.

He was persuaded to attend the special training course for Marine snipers in Virginia.

One hundred and twelve days later, Craig killed his first human being. The man was a senior member of the Taliban who had harboured Bin Laden during the planning stage of the US attack. Craig had been trained to not see a human head in his rifle scope, only an enemy of the United States. Despite it being his first kill, there was no hesitation or nervousness. The Marine training kicked in. One moment the man was shouting at a cowering young woman, the next, he was down. There was no need to confirm the kill. Most of the man's brain was plastered on the faded brick wall behind where he'd been standing. For a microsecond Craig flashed back to the gore splattered on the faded wallpaper in his parents' bedroom. Then it was gone.

The woman who the terrorist had been screaming at was shocked at first, then realising that he was actually dead, began spitting on him and kicking what was left of his face.

Craig had heard a lot of talk during training from other Marines about FKC or First Kill Conscience. He fully expected to feel some remorse or at least disgust for what he'd done, enemy or not. The fact was, the FKC never hit him at all. That night, he ate some decent chow on base, listened to a few tunes then slept like a baby.

Craig had completed two tours in Afghanistan when war broke out (the first time) between the US and Iraq. Craig's skills were desperately needed in what the military knew would end up being an urban, street by street battle.

He was no longer needed for extreme distance single-shot kills. Instead he spent every day in one high-ground position after another as a spotter-killer for convoys and roadblocks.

The Iraq War came with a new kind of home-grown weapon that proved devastating to the US military. The IED (improvised explosive device) became the weapon of choice for the local al-Qaida terrorists. They could be made in a home kitchen from whatever explosive material they could find or concoct. They were usually detonated by cell phone.

The snipers were tasked with looking for suspicious activity on the road where a military convoy was about to pass. These included sidewalks or roadside paths that inexplicably cleared of people and/or a cell phone suddenly being used as a convoy approached. There was a lot of guess work that went on between each sniper and his controller. Getting approval for a kill was based on attack precedent and the growing experience of how the al-Qaida bombers thought.

One day, Craig had the weirdest case of déjà vu he'd ever experienced. He was in the front seat of a Humvee being driven to his next sniper 'perch'. They were in front of a three-vehicle convoy. Craig almost subconsciously noticed an old cereal box abandoned by the side of the road just ahead of them. Before his brain could react, the box exploded.

Even before the shock wave struck the Humvee, Craig screamed "No!" with incredible fury.

He was immediately back on the dirt road. There had been no explosion. Craig was once again looking ahead at the brightly coloured cereal box. He shouted for the driver to stop. He stepped out of the Humvee and retrieved his rifle from the back. He aimed at the box then fired. The box exploded shattering nearby windows. He climbed back into the vehicle and nodded for the driver to continue.

Though the others were looking at him in complete awe, he maintained a look of utter cool. Inside, however, he was trying to get his head around what had just happened. It all still had a dreamlike quality and it was hard to separate which part was the déjà vu and which was the reality. He gave up trying and refocused his mind on the assignment at hand. He was about to make another kill. The déjà vu feeling shouldn't have bothered him, but it did.

The thing was that the terrorists didn't just use men. More and more women were triggering the deadly roadside explosions. Though not ideal, if his shot was approved and the cell user was a young girl, the shot was still taken. If the next convoy passed his rooftop location without being blown apart, it was considered a good kill.

When they started using children, it became real. No US soldier had been trained for that eventuality. Some snipers couldn't take the shot. Some even missed their targets due to the shakes. It wasn't an easy thing to do. Their scopes from the high rooftop vantage points enlarged the children's heads to the point where the shooter could see the freckles and the scared young eyes.

Craig tried to see nothing but potential enemy combatants. When his shot was approved, he only saw a target as his finger tightened on the trigger.

It was only during his second tour of Iraq that something deep within his subconscious finally caught up with him. It started with him feeling the occasional chill. As the heat in Iraq was hardly conducive to having that effect, he at first thought that he might have been getting sick. Like all good soldiers, he chose to ignore it. It wasn't until the first instance of it happening during a sniper operation that he knew something was wrong. The chills were so bad that he actually started to shiver. There was no way he could even sight his target.

He was ordered to see the medic on base. Craig said he was pretty sure he'd caught something. The medic checked him out thoroughly but couldn't find anything physically wrong with him. He asked him whether he was having trouble sleeping, was suffering from any dizzy spells or if he'd started feeling anxiety.

Craig answered no to all the questions. The doctor signed him off as there was nothing he could see that was wrong with him. He did, however, make a small note in Craig's file that he was on his fourth tour on sniper detail. One of the most stressful assignments in-country.

After a few weeks, the chills seemed to ease off a bit. Craig joined his unit for the regular Saturday movie night. That week it was Adam Sandler's Fifty First Dates. The place was packed. Not because of Sandler but because Drew Barrymore was a favourite among the Marines.

Halfway through the movie, when they showed Drew's character's family having to restage their entire home every night so she could re-live the same day, Craig started to cry. Craig never cried. He hardly ever shed a tear even as a child and he certainly never turned on the waterworks as a fucking Marine.

He tried to will it to stop but he found he had no control over his emotions whatsoever. Tears streamed down his face. When the movie ended with Drew waking up on board a sailboat in the middle of a glacial bay, he started sobbing.

Hard.

This time the doctors had no trouble diagnosing the problem. Craig had a record of sixty-one kills during his four tours. At no time had he shown any emotional reaction to any of the shootings, including those that involved women and especially children. Like all snipers, Craig had built a wall around his emotions.

That wall was now starting to crumble. The military hadn't yet become comfortable with the term PTSD (post-traumatic stress disorder), but the doctor could recognise the symptoms a mile away.

Craig was ordered back to Pendleton for restricted duty, R and R and some time with the base shrink. Craig knew in his heart that he'd be back in the 'show' in no time.

Craig wasn't aware of the fact that any Marine who'd had a documented mental breakdown put in his file, would never hold a sniper position again. The military's feeling was that if there was any chance of you going crazy, placing you on a rooftop with one of the most powerful and accurate rifles in their arsenal hardly sounded like a good idea, even to those who managed the business of death.

When Craig learned that the closest he would ever get to being a sniper again was to become a trainer for the next generation, he was devastated. He had been making a real difference for his country and now they were going to just put him out to pasture.

Craig started drinking. At first it was just a couple of cold ones with his friends, then in almost record time it became more than just a social thing. He found that the alcohol took the edge off the hurt and guilt he was feeling inside. The problem wasn't because of guilt for the lives he'd taken, but rather for the lives he could no longer take. He continued his sessions with the base's specialist on PTSD (without calling it that) during the day. At night he continued his own personal brand of therapy at a loud and raunchy dive bar by the coast road in Oceanside.

He started to realise in his booze-addled mind that drinking away his problems with beer was just plain stupid. It took too long and cost too much. He moved on to shots between brews. Just like his birth dad (flowers and wine evolving to the jug) the beer gave way to ever larger quantities of cheap tequila.

He was on the road to self-destruction either through alcohol poisoning or a head-on collision as he veered his way back to the base. The booze did its job and cleared his head of any troubling thoughts or anxieties, but the mornings were becoming tougher to bear. Fellow Marines started to avoid him. They could pick up the signs of a burn-out and didn't want to be anywhere close when the crash came. He still managed to find some who'd drink with him. Other Marines that were on their way to reaching the same critical mass.

Craig had arrived at a point when there were moments, brief ones, but moments all the same, when he considered ending all his troubles with his personal Smith and Wesson. The only thing stopping him was the thought of what Julie would go through when she learned of his suicide. Craig knew that she would blame herself and that was something he couldn't let happen. He already felt terrible that he hadn't been home in ages and rarely talked to her on WhatsApp any more since the tequila took over.

Then the strangest thing happened. He went into San Diego with a bunch of the guys who liked to drink like grown-ups (the jug). They went bar-hopping in the Gaslamp District and ended up at a weird New York-themed bar which was full of UCSD students who were in town for a convention.

He ended up in a drinking competition with one girl who stood out from the rest. Sure, she was pretty and had a body and all, but there was something else. She had poise.

She had a certain dignity, even as she matched him shot for shot. It was like she knew what the hell she was doing and always would.

It was hard to tell between the Marines and the students as to who were the rowdiest. Between them, they managed to clear out most of the other customers. At some point a darts challenge was made. The students creamed the hardened soldiers. They hardly won a game. Not willing to be bested by a bunch of art students, they challenged them to a sport in which they were unlikely to lose.

It was a straight drinking game. Each contender had to down a Cuervo Gold shot. They then had to balance the shot glass on their head and walk to the end of the room. The problem was that the Marines had been knocking it back for hours before even arriving at the bar and had done so on empty stomachs. The uni bunch had sensibly eaten burgers and fries before hitting the town.

Four shots into the competition and some of the boys in green started having trouble. By the sixth round most of them were finding it difficult to walk at all, never mind balancing a glass on their head. All except Craig. His eyes may have looked a little glassy but to an onlooker, the tequila didn't appear to be affecting him at all.

By the eighth round, both teams were looking pretty rough. There were only three competitors left. Two from UCSD, and Craig. After downing the shots, one of the UCSD kids darted to the men's room with his hand over his mouth holding back what was surely going to be some prodigious vomiting.

That left only two. Though Craig seemed outwardly unfazed by the amount of alcohol he'd consumed, inside, he was actually feeling hammered. He eyed the sole opponent and recognised for the first time that she was a woman and a pretty hot one at that.

Craig introduced himself making sure that he didn't slur his words or barf. Jenny Reed did the same.

It took two more rounds for the victor to be crowned. Jenny accepted the trophy (an empty shot glass) with great humility as Craig watched her with a goofy smile on his face.

He woke up next to her in a cheap chain hotel a few blocks from the bar. Jenny was still clothed. He wasn't. At some point he'd hurled outside the bar and she had rented a room, cleaned him up and put him to bed.

He looked at her through puffy, red-rimmed eyes. "Did we fuck?" he asked gallantly.

"Oh god yes. It was a fantasy night. What with the vomit and the passing out – it was every woman's dream," she replied.

"You threw up?"

"Not me, you idiot – you!" She shook her head. "Why don't you get up, brush your teeth – twice, then let's get some breakfast."

They started seeing each other casually about once every couple of weeks. Then it became weekly. Craig started to realise that the more he saw of Jenny, the less he felt the need to deaden his emotions.

That wasn't to say that he didn't still feel the draw and sneak back occasionally to the Oceanside dump, but the craving diminished. He started to listen to the shrink and made more of an effort to actually talk to him.

He asked Jenny one day what the hell she could possibly see in a burned-out alcoholic Marine. She looked him in the eyes and said, "I see the you before you were ever a Marine. Before you experienced some of the real evils that mankind can do to each other. That's what I see in you. I can also see that we are going to have a great life together."

He was stunned. He had never even considered such a possibility. The idea that Gunnery Sergeant Craig Edmonds might actually end up being loved by somebody. He smiled back at her.

"You know what? That wouldn't be half bad."

CHAPTER
FOURTEEN

What would end up being one of the worst days in Craig's life started perfectly normally. There was the usual bathroom chaos and a rushed breakfast followed by the kids playing in the living room. Jenny spent an hour in her tiny adjoining 'office' to catch up on any overnight emails concerning her fledgling graphic art business.

Jenny had found the perfect niche for her talent while at the same time not having to send the kids off to day-care while she spent her days in a claustrophobic office. She knew that she never wanted to work for an agency again. That part was easy. Her time with Harris Barker Graphics had been a demoralising and frustrating experience. She felt as if she was working in a factory, churning out media without any regard for quality or artistic merit. While she tried to work out what exactly she wanted to do, she got a call from a friend who was about to self-publish a children's book. She asked if Jenny would be interested in doing the cover art and a few of the story illustrations.

Since that fateful day, she began specialising in creating custom book-cover art for self-publishers. She had never been happier. She could stay at home with the kids and work around their schedules while being able to keep her artistic juices flowing freely. The money wasn't bad either.

When Craig got to work he checked his email and found that he'd received a reply from Salt Lake City about the funky camera footage. The tech rambled on about the technical stuff she'd tried – all of which might as well have been Chinese to Craig. He was not a very technically-minded person and trying to read about pixel isolation and reverse compression interpolation was enough to give him the beginnings of a headache.

He scrolled to the end of the outpouring and saw that there were two attachments. One video and one JPEG. He opened the video file. It was the camera video from HWY 89 before the truck arrived at their house. He again saw the few recognisable vehicles that had passed the camera then reached the part that had been too dark to see anything. The video was grainy but the tech had managed to bring out an image that wasn't perceivable before. Craig thought he would be delighted to get more information about the truck, but what he saw was unsettling.

The vehicle that was now visible was indeed the truck he'd seen driving away from the house. Craig guessed it to have been manufactured in the 1950s judging by the curved hood and rounded wheel arches. The outline of the vehicle seemed to glow in the dark. The thing looked strangely spectral.

The part that gave Craig a shot of ice down his spine was that the driver was old beyond human capacity. A faded Texaco hat was perched above a face that looked skeletal. The skin was so thin that Craig could see the outline of facial bones. The topper was that the driver was smiling showing a mouth full of too many yellowed teeth. The thin leathery lips were drawn back revealing black gums where the teeth were anchored into the jaw bones.

"Jesus," Craig exclaimed before he could stop himself. He checked that he was still alone in the office. He tried to avoid ever swearing or blaspheming when at work. It was not the LDS way.

Once he got over the pure weirdness of the image, his instinct returned and he tried to find any identifying logo or licence plate on the vintage truck.

The angle was wrong to see the side view of the cargo area. The licence plate however was visible, but Craig had never seen one quite like it. It was black with raised white numbers and letters. It read 494 NRB. He felt that at least with it being so unusual, it would be easier to trace.

Gary Clarkson walked in as Craig was entering the licence plate details into the nationwide tracing site.

"Hey," Gary said as he sat at the desk in front of Craig's.

"Hey," Craig replied.

"That was a bad one yesterday, wasn't it?" Craig said.

"Just about as bad as they come. I couldn't get to sleep for the longest time."

"Me too," Craig added as he surreptitiously closed the tracing app. "Do you remember a really old Native American guy watching the goings-on yesterday at the accident site?" Craig asked.

"Can't say as I do, but I was kind of focused on what they were bringing up that hill," Gary replied.

"I get that. I was only asking because the guy showed up at my front door just after dinner."

"The old Indian guy?"

"Yup," Craig answered.

"What'd he want?"

"He was spouting a bunch of nonsense about insane animals and mirrors. I sent him on his way... that reminds me, he said he lives out at the end of Old Mesa Road. I didn't think anyone lived out there?"

"That's 'cause they don't," Gary stated. "The road got washed out... must be ten years ago. There weren't any homes out there then anyway and there sure as heck haven't been any built since the road got took. It's just wild sage brush and sidewinders. I think the guy may have given you a bad address."

"Yeah. That's what I thought."

Craig's computer screen came back to life with a pop-up that stated that he was using the wrong site to search for United Kingdom registration plates. It gave him a link to UK site but advised that if he wasn't an authorised UK police official he would not be able to use the website.

"Great," Craig mumbled as he logged off.

Jenny took a break from the computer and gave Tim and Sally a single cookie and a glass of milk each. She sat at the kitchen table while they had their afternoon treat. She listened to their stories and thoughts as she tried to continue her first attempt at knitting a scarf. She had only just taken up the hobby and so far couldn't understand why peopled referred to it as a stress reliever. It was driving her mad. The knitting kit that Craig found for her in St George had instructions that were easy to follow, but for some reason she couldn't seem to get the hang of it. She'd had to undo two false starts already. She was growing to hate the beautiful forest green yarn that Craig had picked out for her.

The moment the kids finished the cookies and milk, they charged into the living room to play. She couldn't understand how two small children could make so much noise when running; then again it wasn't as if their playing was that quiet either. Sally was usually the first to start screaming when she felt that Tim had done her egregious harm like taking a Lego piece that she was about to use or, God forbid, something truly intolerable like using one of her colouring pencils without asking.

The 'good' thing, if that's the right word, about having the kids at home all day was that their din began to fade into the background and was no more jarring than the sound of birdsong. Well, almost.

What was really jarring was when they stopped making noise as had just occurred. The sudden silence was so unique in a house with two young children, that alarm bells went off in Jenny's head before she even knew why.

Her first reaction as she walked into the living room was that they were playing a game. They were both sitting bolt upright on the couch staring straight ahead.

"What are you playing?"

As she passed the mirror she distinctly felt a draft come from it. She turned towards it and was faced with what looked like a dark, damp tunnel. A dense ground fog obscured the floor. Jenny stumbled back as she saw that the grey mist wasn't just in the mirror. It was swirling out of the frame and into her living room.

She took another step back. Two sinewy and withered arms enveloped her from behind. She could feel hot breath on her neck. It smelled of decay. She heard a weak, gravelly whisper.

"It is mine you are now. Sleep the sleep of the dead."

Jenny felt as if she was rising in the air and was being guided towards the mirror, then there was nothing.

Craig turned off HWY 89 onto Johnson Canyon Road and after a mile, looked for the house lights as he always did during the winter months. He tried to get out of the office before five when there was a faint bit of daylight remaining, but that day the written questions about the Glendale accident arrived from the NTSB and they wanted the two attending officers to complete the forms immediately.

A chill went through Craig's body when he couldn't see the lights. Their house was on an upwards slope and was visible, if you knew where to look, from the road. He unconsciously pressed down harder on the gas. He didn't consider himself a worrier but there was no good reason for the house to be in darkness with a woman and two children inside unless something was wrong.

The fuse! He realised there was in fact a good reason. Well, not a good one but at least one that made some sense. If the fuse had gone again, Jen would wait for him to get home and fix it. She would be prepared for them to get by with candles and camping lights for an hour.

He wondered, if that was the case, shouldn't he be able to see the candlelight from the road?

He turned into their drive and pulled up to the front door. He was glad that his Explorer had the sixty-second delay before its headlights switched off. He needed the light to get to the door.

He swung it open and knew immediately that something was wrong. It wasn't just because he expected to see wrong every day in his job, it was more like the feel of the house had changed. It had always felt like home when he walked through the door after work. There would be cooking smells and noise. Lots of noise.

All he could smell was the scent of old woodsmoke from the previous day's fire plus a back odour of something rotten. There was no trace of cooking and no sound whatsoever.

He drew his gun as he reached for the hall light switch, though he wasn't expecting anything to happen. He flipped the switch.

The lights came on.

He walked into the kitchen and was able to turn those lights on as well. Nothing was out of place which was a mixed sign. An immaculate kitchen was not a good thing to see at 6pm on a work night. Jenny was usually in the middle of dinner prep by then.

He backed out of the room and slowly approached the living room. He stopped and listened. He felt a presence in the room.

He turned on the light.

"Dear God!"

Tim and Sally were sitting bolt upright on the sofa. Their eyes were wide open as they stared blankly straight ahead. He ran to them and dropped to his knees. He checked their skin and it felt normal. He looked into their eyes and they too looked as they usually did except they didn't appear to see him or even be aware that he was right in front of them.

He waved his hand in front of their eyes. They didn't blink. He took their pulses and felt a heartbeat for both of them. It was slow but steady. If he didn't know better he would have thought they were sleeping. Then again, kids, normal healthy kids, don't sleep sitting bolt upright with their eyes wide open. He checked them further and noticed that both had a damp patch on their jeans. They were way too old for that kind of accident. Craig, now getting even more frantic, rubbed his fingers against the dark area then smelled them. It was definitely urine.

"Jenny!" he called out.

There was no answering call.

"Jenny!" he shouted louder.

Still nothing.

He left the kids where they were and did a quick search of the house and its perimeter all the while shouting out Jenny's name. Inside, everything looked normal in a messy mid-afternoon way. Toys hadn't been picked up yet. Jenny hadn't made the bed yet. But other than that, nothing unusual.

He walked back into the living room and as he was passing the mirror, something caught his eye. It was a small length of the forest green yarn that Jen had been using to try and learn how to knit. It was on the carpet in front of the mirror. Craig bent and tried to pick it up.

The colour drained from his face as he stumbled backwards. His stress chills were back. He could feel the sensation gathering at the base of his spine. He knew that it would soon begin to creep higher. He could hear the sound of his rapid stress breathing.

He knelt by the mirror and looked more closely at the small length of yarn. One end was on the floor. The other end was on the mirror, only it wasn't on the mirror. That's what terrified him. The other end of the yarn went through the mirror. Six inches from the bottom, the yarn was sticking out of the reflective glass. Craig tried to pull it but it was held fast within the mirror's surface.

It was almost as if the yarn had been dangling into water as it froze. The mirror of course wasn't water and wasn't frozen. As he stared at the piece of yarn, he also noticed a small area of discolouration on one bit of the frame directly under the green wool. He switched on his phone light and examined it closely. Careful not to destroy potential evidence, he grabbed a toothpick from the kitchen and lightly touched the spot. It was almost dry but not quite. Against the light wood of the toothpick, he could see that the substance was red. Blood red.

Craig's thoughts went back to the old man. Ahote. He'd asked if they'd received the portal yet. Craig suddenly understood that the man hadn't been crazy at all and that they had received it. Not only had they received it, but someone or something had taken Jenny through it.

He sat in the deafening silence of his home and was at a loss. It wasn't just about the children or about Jenny. It was that he had no idea what to do. He knew he had to call for help but didn't imagine that whole scenario going well. Husbands who claim their wives have been taken away by supernatural beings are unlikely to be believed and would probably move up to position one on the suspect list.

A gust of winter wind shook the house and he heard the front door bang against the wall. He had forgotten to shut it properly. He got to his feet and walked down the hall. He took hold of the door handle and started to swing it shut.

He saw something in his peripheral vision charging towards him.

CHAPTER
FIFTEEN

Before Craig had a chance to turn, Steeler ran right into him. He started whining and head-butting Craig's thigh. He seemed frantic as he ran down the hall towards the living room. He slowed as he gave the mirror a wide berth then made his way to the sofa. He stopped in front of Tim and placed his right paw on Tim's knees. There was no reaction. He did the same to Sally but she too remained motionless. Steeler lowered himself to the ground and lay in front of the children. It was obvious that he had no intention of leaving them alone again.

Craig used the landline to call the Kane County sheriff. Cliff Walsh was in his late sixties and had been sheriff for almost thirty years. He was a good sheriff. After all those years, he had nothing to prove which kept him immune from influence when the town council occasionally tried to pressure him into leaning this way or that.

He listened as Craig described what he'd seen since he got home. He left out anything that sounded remotely supernatural, though he did mention the old man who'd come to his door. He'd asked about him in the office so it wouldn't have looked good to omit him now. Also, though he somehow doubted it, Ahote could himself be the abductor.

Walsh told him to sit tight and to not touch a thing. Craig's next call was to Julie. She was shocked to hear about what was going on and said she would get up there as soon as she could.

Craig had of course known not to touch anything in the house as it was about to become a crime scene. He bent the rules slightly and placed a blanket over the laps of his two catatonic children. He desperately wanted to grab each of them and hug the situation better but he knew that things were way past a hug being the answer. He also wanted to get them into clean, dry clothes but he knew that they could possibly have trace evidence on them and also couldn't be touched.

Craig heard the sirens a few minutes before the county vehicles pulled up in front of the house.

Craig looked at his co-workers and friends as they stepped out of their SUVs. He saw the hardened expressions of their faces. He knew, as most Americans who watch the news did, that husbands whose wives mysteriously disappear almost always end up being responsible for their disappearance. Craig understood that his fellow officers were likely to already be suspecting him.

He wished he could be more forthcoming with all the details, but a modern-day investigator was not likely to accept concepts like portals and alternate dimensions. Not that Craig had fully drunk that Kool-Aid either. He still had hope that Jenny would walk in with a perfectly good explanation as to where she'd been. Of course, the condition of his kids made that outcome seem less likely by the minute. Kids don't go into zombie mode just cause Mom has stepped out for a minute, not that Jen would ever leave them unattended in the house for even a second.

Craig tried to think what he would feel if he was called to a house where the wife was missing and the children appeared to be in shock, almost as if they had seen something so horrible their little minds had closed down rather than process the data. He knew he would suspect the husband of foul play almost immediately.

The only thing that might give pause to such linear thinking was the piece of yarn. There was no rational explanation for that. As he escorted the officers and paramedics into the living room he surreptitiously glanced down at the mirror. He felt the chill stir and rise further up his spine.

The piece of yarn was gone.

So was the blood.

The paramedics examined Tim and Sally but could find nothing wrong with either of them. They considered taking them to the Kane County Hospital, but advised that there was no staff child psychologist on duty and that they might end up having to go to St George. Sheriff Walsh stepped in and suggested they stay with their father for the time being at least until they had a few answers as to what happened. He didn't feel that moving the kids all around Southern Utah was the best thing to do for them at that moment. He also knew that by taking them away from Craig, a deputy sheriff, it would cause so much negative tongue-wagging in town that Craig would likely as not be found guilty by the court of public opinion before the sun even came up.

What had also helped Walsh make the decision to leave the kids with Craig was when he heard that their grandmother was on her way. That statement made everyone feel much more comfortable. They all knew Julie and her reputation and skill with children.

Deputies checked Jenny's office and saw that her laptop was open but sleeping. They woke it up and saw a split screen. One showed what looked like a book cover that was in mid design, the other screen was her Gmail home page. They opened her outbox and saw that she had sent quite a few emails throughout the day but the last one was at 3:27 pm. They opened one email in her drafts folder and saw that it was incomplete. It showed it last being opened at 3:29 pm. The deputies were both computer literate but were hardly expert at going deep into the OS and bringing up use-time logs. They did, however, have the bright idea of opening Time Machine and checking back to when the book cover had last been modified.

That had occurred at 3:25 pm. It seemed that Jenny had stopped work just before 3:30. The question was whether it was voluntary or not. They had hoped to find her cell phone but had no success.

Sheriff Walsh asked for a quiet place where he could question Craig. They decided on the kitchen. It was a strange feeling when the noisiest room in the house became the quiet place to talk.

Walsh knew that he needed to interview Craig as a possible suspect but he was having trouble correlating the timeline. The sheriff had seen Craig leave the office only forty minutes before he called him to report Jenny missing. He also knew that Craig had been at the office all day except when he and Gary had gone out on a call in the morning.

If Jenny was still working up to 3:30 and Craig didn't leave the office till gone six, he didn't see a time slot where he could have come home, removed his wife in such a way as to have scared the children into shock, while leaving no evidence of violence, a struggle or a body.

He asked Craig to go through every moment from the time he left the office until he called to report the disappearance. Craig first told Walsh about the visit from the old man the night before and how he had been rambling about the family being in danger and that Craig could find him at the end of Old Mesa Road. He also told the sheriff about the man's parting words telling them to look into Jenny's family history and any disappearances that may have occurred every twenty-five years.

"Bud?" the sheriff called out.

One of the older deputies stepped into the kitchen.

"Who do we have at the south end of town tonight?" Walsh asked.

"Bill Harris is at the airport checking out that report of kids with drones," Bud replied.

"Give him a call and ask him to go out to Old Mesa Road…" Walsh began.

"That road's been closed for years," Bud interrupted.

"I'm well aware of that. Just tell him to go to the end of the road."

Walsh turned to Craig. "That's what he said, right? The end of the road?"

Craig nodded. Walsh looked back at Bud. "Tell him to go have a look right away."

"You got it, Cliff."

Once Bud was gone, Craig took him through his movements from the time he left the office and drove home. He told him about there being no lights on and about finding the kids in that condition. He described his searching the property for Jenny, even about Steeler almost knocking him over to get into the house. That part seemed to interest him.

"Is the dog usually left outside all day?" he asked.

"Definitely not. Especially in the winter. The poor guy would freeze. No, he goes out for a morning mooch and does his business then usually gets let out again mid-afternoon, then again for a quick walk just before bed."

"So that's another piece of the time puzzle. Sounds to me that whatever happened occurred when Steeler was outside for his mid-afternoon jaunt and didn't get let back in," Walsh surmised.

"That makes sense, I guess," Craig agreed.

The sheriff took a deep breath before he continued.

"I've got to ask you some questions that you're not gonna like, but I know that you'll understand the reason why."

"Because as her husband, I am the prime suspect," Craig stated flatly.

"Unfortunately, that is the case, but to be honest with you, I'm not feeling it. Still, I have to ask 'em."

The sheriff enquired about how their marriage was doing. Were they fighting? Were there money problems? Walsh wrote down all the answers though he knew them before he asked. Jenny and Craig were the happiest couple in Kanab. They had everyone over in the spring and fall for huge barbeques and there had never been even the slightest sign of trouble.

The only thing that kept creeping back into the sheriff's head was Craig's background in the Marines and subsequent PTSD. He had taken a risk when he hired him but he'd got a feel about the guy when they first met. Craig had been completely open about his condition and the subsequent treatment. He told him about the meds he took and even the booster pills he had in case he felt the world closing in on him again.

Craig hadn't made him doubt his decision even once. Craig was a solid family man and a damn good deputy.

Bud knocked on the kitchen door frame.

"What ya got?" Walsh asked.

"Harris just called back. He made it almost a mile on the old road but only got as far as where it got washed away. It's dark but he used his spotlight to see if there was any way to cross the wash. He said there wasn't. There's a ten-foot drop on either side where the water took everything with it."

"Thanks, Bud."

"Looks like the old man sold you a bill of goods," Walsh said as he looked back at Craig. "We'll keep an eye out for an old man in an old Jeep, though that ain't exactly an unusual description around here. Heck! That sounds like half of the population of Fredonia."

Craig forced a smile and nodded his agreement.

The sheriff was about to say something else when another deputy put his head around the corner.

"Sheriff, you may want to see this."

Walsh raised his eyebrows at Craig then got to his feet.

"Should I stay here?" Craig asked.

"No. You might as well come and find out what the boys have found. It's your house."

Craig followed them down the hall and saw that they were donning their winter coats. He followed suit and stepped out into the frigid night air. The deputy led them to the side of the house. Craig suddenly knew where they were going and felt his heart rate quicken. Two other deputies were standing at the fuse box. The metal door was open and both were shining their flashlights into the box. His winter coat was still on the ground where he'd left it after the spider incident.

Walsh walked up to the box and took a good look inside. It wasn't hard for Paul to guess what his deputies had found. The home-made flamethrower had left a black layer of soot over most of the box's interior. The sheriff wiped a finger across one area. The tip of his finger was black. He turned to Craig.

"Mind explaining this?"

"That happened yesterday," Craig explained. "We lost power and when I came to check the fuse, there was a black widow nest inside the fuse box."

"Most people would think to use a broom. Not a… actually, what the heck did you use?" Walsh asked.

Before Craig could answer, Bud appeared from the workshop carrying the aerosol can, the gloves and the matches.

Craig could do nothing but shrug his shoulders. "That's what I used."

Walsh looked at the items then back at Craig. "Home-made flamethrower. You're lucky you didn't burn the house down. Or was that the intent?"

Craig gave him a 'you must be kidding' look.

"I used fire because I hate spiders. There was no way I was going to try a broom. They could just as easily crawl up the handle. The flamethrower was much more efficient and I could keep my distance."

"I hope you can understand my immediate concern. You talk about coming home to a dark house and we find signs of malicious activity at the fuse box plus what looks like a perfectly good coat lying in the dirt."

"It had spiders on it," Craig mumbled.

"Hmmm." The sheriff didn't look completely convinced.

Craig stared him down. "Jenny being missing and my putting flames to a spider's nest are unrelated. You just told me that there was no way within the time frame for me to be responsible for Jenny's disappearance."

"There's still no way you could have been with me in the office and out here kidnapping your wife unless you tampered with the evidence. Maybe you controlled her computer from work." He turned to the deputies. "What's that called when you control one computer from another?"

"Remote access," one of them answered.

"That's easy enough to check," Craig pointed out. "If you really want to verify the timeline, check the landline records for the phone in Jen's office. That's her business line. She must make twenty calls a day. Check it out."

"Already in the works. Shame we can't find her cell phone."

"She hardly ever used it for work. The reception's not great out here and our carrier doesn't permit Wi-Fi calling. Hence the landlines. One for the house and one for her business."

"What happens when you call her cell?" Walsh asked.

Craig looked back at his superior with utter dismay.

"You haven't tried, have you?"

"It never even dawned on me," Craig answered as he shook his head in self-disgust.

"Almost like you knew nobody would answer," Walsh mentioned.

Craig could only shake his head in frustration.

Walsh whipped out his cell. "What's her number?"

Craig gave it to him and watched as he dialled. Walsh finished entering the numbers then held the phone to his ear. He looked impatiently at the screen.

"I got no signal." He put the cell back in his shirt pocket. "We've pretty much done all we can up here in the dark. I'm gonna call it a night but understand that we'll be back in the morning if she hasn't turned up. We'll probably bring dogs."

The sheriff studied Craig's face closely as he said those last words.

"That's a good idea," Craig replied.

"I'll be trying her phone as soon as I get a signal," Walsh said as he was getting into his SUV. "Don't try calling it yourself until I call you. Understand?"

"Absolutely."

"Oh, one more thing. I'm leaving one deputy up here. He'll leave when your mother arrives. That's the only way I can justify allowing the children to remain in the house."

"I don't understand. The house isn't a crime scene," Craig insisted.

"No, it's not. But if Jenny doesn't come back or the dogs find something, then it's very possible that it could become one," Walsh replied.

"I didn't kill my wife, Sheriff."

"I want to believe you. Tell the deputy if the children's condition changes."

Craig watched as the crew piled into their various vehicles and headed down his drive. The second they reached Johnson Canyon Road, Craig walked slowly to the back of his property, to one specific spot. It was the only place on his ten acres where you could always count on getting a signal. He pressed the home button and told Siri to call Jenny.

Her phone rang but she didn't answer. He tried a second time for no other reason than he didn't know what else to do. It rang again but still no one answered.

He shoved the phone into his pocket and headed back to the house. Before he even reached the front door he could hear Steeler whining and barking from somewhere inside. The deputy was parked halfway along the drive and had his engine running and windows up to stave off the cold. He couldn't hear a thing. Craig found Steeler on the upstairs landing facing a blank wall as he continued to bark and cry.

Craig stroked the confused Lab on the head then made for the living room. He suddenly heard a very familiar piece of music. It was Elton John's '*I Guess That's Why They Call It the Blues*'. The song was so familiar because it was Jenny's cell phone ringtone. He followed the sound. It seemed to be coming from upstairs. He could also hear Steeler getting even loonier. The song stopped. Craig stopped midway up the stairs. After a few moments it restarted. Obviously the sheriff was trying to call it again. Craig made it to the landing and, once he moved Steeler aside, listened with his ear against the wall.

The music was much clearer. It was coming from inside the wall.

'*I guess that's why they call it the blues.*'

CHAPTER
SIXTEEN

The landline began ringing. There was little doubt who was calling. Craig answered the extension in their bedroom. The sheriff's voice boomed though the earpiece.

"I tried twice. No answer. I don't suppose it rang somewhere in the house?"

"I certainly didn't hear it," Craig lied.

"Okay, I'll see you tomorrow. Try to get some sleep."

Craig stared down at his phone as he felt his stomach do a backflip. He had never lied to the sheriff before. It's never a good thing to lie to your supervisor. Doing so when you're a suspect in the possible abduction of your wife is definitely not a good plan. The fact was that he didn't feel like telling him that he had heard the phone, but it was coming from inside a wall. He could tell him that later. First of all, Craig needed to know what it all meant.

He took the wireless landline phone with him back onto the landing. He dialled the number. Elton John returned. Craig moved his ear along the wall till the tone was the clearest. He tapped the wall. He already knew that it was solid brick. They'd found that out when they tried to hammer a picture hook onto the same wall. Three bent nails later, he'd had to fetch his drill.

The other side of the wall was in Tim's room. He took a look from there. It was still just a wall. It was solid brick. There was no secret crawl space, no HVAC ducting, no cables, nothing. Just solid brick. Yet the sound of Jenny's phone was coming from within that wall.

Craig wanted nothing more than to get his sledgehammer and make absolutely sure, but he suspected that destroying a wall when the police are looking for your wife could be another of those subtle red flags.

He went back downstairs to check on the kids. When he'd been outside with the sheriff, a female officer had removed their clothes as evidence and had cleaned them up with some wet wipes before dressing them in pyjamas she'd found in their rooms.

Their eyes were closed which Craig took as a good sign. Their breathing was regular and their colour was good. He gently lay them down on their end of the sectional sofa and made sure the blanket covered them, leaving just their heads exposed. He kissed them both on the forehead then sat on the other end of the couch where he could watch them. Steeler joined the family and staked himself out halfway between father and children.

At one point Craig could hear Jenny's ringtone again but didn't bother to get up. He checked his watch and saw that it was past one in the morning. He wanted to stay awake but he could feel the pull of sleep trying to drag him down and away from the conscious reality.

He fought the urge to close his eyes.

He then heard a scraping noise come from the kitchen, closely followed by Steeler scrambling to his feet and charging out of the room. Steeler began barking madly.

Craig was still wearing his uniform and hadn't even put his gun in the locker. He got to his feet and removed the gun from its holster. He kept the weapon at his side.

He stood by the kitchen doorway and listened. Steeler had stopped barking but he could hear strange sounds coming from the utility room. Craig crept to the open door then, in one fluid move, he raised the gun, stepped into the doorway and turned on the light.

He was stunned at the vision in front of him. Julie was on her knees rubbing Steeler's tummy. He had gone silent because he was in a happy trance. His legs each pointed in a different direction. His mouth was wide open with his tongue lolling out the left side.

"I know that this is the only thing that stops him barking. I was trying to sneak in without waking everyone." Julie smiled up at him. "You can put the gun away now."

"How the hell did you get here so fast?"

"It's a six-hour drive. I took six hours. What's the big deal?"

"I didn't realise you were going to head out the moment you put the phone down," Craig said.

"Well, you should have. You know me well enough. Is there any news? How are the kids?"

"Everything's the same; we're all camped out in the living room."

"Then will you please put down the gun and put on a pot of coffee while I check on them. Then you are going to tell me exactly what's been happening. Not that redacted nonsense you gave me over the phone." Julie got to her feet and gave Craig a hug before going to see her grandchildren.

Craig looked down at Steeler and smiled. The goofy beast was still on his back with a look of pure ecstasy on his face. Craig shook his head and after putting the Glock back in the safe, he went into the kitchen to make coffee.

He brought two mugs into the living room.

"They look like they're just sleeping," Julie said.

"I know. If they don't come around tomorrow we're going to have to take them to the hospital just so they can get liquids and nourishment."

"Have you tried to feed them anything?"

"Actually, no," Craig admitted. "I just assumed they couldn't eat or drink."

Julie gave him one of her raised eyebrow looks.

"We'll give it a try in the morning. They seem to be sleeping peacefully now," she said.

"I'm not sure that's sleep."

"Whatever it is, they seem peaceful," Julie added as she took a sip from her mug. "Do you want to tell me what's really going on or am I supposed to guess?"

Craig spent the next hour telling her everything that had happened over the past few days. He didn't hold anything back. When he finished, she asked him to call Jenny's phone so she could hear it ring in the wall.

He used the landline and in a moment, Jenny's ringtone could be heard from upstairs. Julie followed the sound then called down to Craig.

"Didn't you say it was coming from the wall on the landing?"

Craig ran upstairs and dialled her number again using the wireless phone from the bedroom. The music was no longer coming from the same place. It was coming from the ceiling above the master bedroom.

"I think we need to check out the attic," Julie stated flatly.

"You heard what I told you about the last time I looked up there."

"So, what are you saying?" Julie insisted. "We should just let your missing wife's phone ring without checking it out, just because of a few animals?"

Craig gave her a piercing stare.

"Okay, maybe it was more than just a few," she relented.

"I'll get the ladder," he replied.

Craig was back within minutes. He handed Julie a flashlight then went through the same difficulties fitting the ladder into the bathroom while angling it up to the opening. He gave Julie one long glare, grabbed the flashlight then took a deep breath before climbing up to the hatch. He slid back the bolt then pressed both his hands against the wooden insert.

"You'll catch me if I fall?" he half-joked.

"Don't I always?" she replied.

Craig grunted as he applied pressure to the wooden square. It finally began to lift. He held it in that position for a moment and listened. He couldn't hear a thing. He lifted it out of the square opening and slid it into the attic. He slowly poked his head through the opening. He again listened. There wasn't a sound.

After his previous experience, he opted to not reach up for the switch without knowing what was waiting for him; rather he would use the LED flashlight which was much brighter anyway. He turned it on and shone it across the attic.

It took him a moment for his brain to understand what he was actually looking at. It was no longer the dusty attic that he had seen a few days earlier. The walls were curved and covered in something wet. It dawned on him with revulsion that it looked a little like the images he had seen on TV from a colonoscopy camera. As he looked on in horror, he saw that the wet ooze was actually moving. Whatever he was looking at seemed to be alive.

"What do you see?" Julie called up at him.

"I'm not sure. I just want to…"

As he eased a little further up, the light from his flashlight dropped lower onto what should have been the attic floor. Craig couldn't see the floor. There might have been one but it was completely obscured by the hundreds of rattlesnakes that were entwined with each other as they slowly slithered like one organised mass. As if on cue, they all started to rattle at the same time. The sound was overwhelming.

Craig almost did fall off the ladder. Just like the previous visit to the attic, Craig desperately scrambled to get the wooden hatch plate back in position and the locking bolt into its receptacle.

"What's the matter?" Julie sounded concerned.

"Do you remember the original movie *Poltergeist*?"

"Sure. Fun and scary," Julie replied.

"Do you remember the scene when the little girl's bedroom closet bursts open and there is this throat thing

148

trying to pull her in?" Craig asked as he tried to catch his breath.

"Vaguely," she answered.

"Well, it's in our attic! Oh yeah, and we have snakes."

She stared at him with concern.

"Are you still going to treatment?" she asked.

"This is nothing to do with my PTSD. Something took Jenny and I think they're somehow both still in the house."

"If that's the case, then we can find them," Julie announced excitedly.

"When I said they are in the house, I meant they are literally part of the house."

Before Julie could reply, Craig grabbed her by the arm and looked into her worried face.

"I need you to look after the kids. I have to go out."

"What? It's two in the morning," she exclaimed.

"I'm starting to believe that there's only one person that may know how to get Jen back."

"That nice sheriff I spoke to?"

"No. The old man. Ahote. He seemed to know that all this was going to happen," Craig said. "I don't know how long I'll be gone."

She looked for any of the signs of his being in the midst of a relapse but, despite the lunacy of what they had been discussing, she felt he knew what he was doing.

"Bring her back."

Craig kissed her on the cheek then turned to go.

"Shit!"

"What?" she asked.

"The sheriff left a deputy to stay on the property. I doubt he's gonna let me leave."

"I spoke to him when I arrived. He was only instructed to stay till I got here. He's gone now."

Craig took a deep breath then blew it out in relief. He gave her a positive nod then ran down the stairs. He grabbed his coat, his keys and his Glock.

CHAPTER
SEVENTEEN

He didn't pass another car on the drive into Kanab. The night was moonless and black. The first lights he saw were those of the town. He turned left onto 89A and headed south. The closer he got to the turn off for Old Mesa Road, the more he started to feel like a complete idiot. The sheriff had confirmed that the road wasn't just closed, it was gone. Washed away by a hundred-year flood that took place over ten years ago.

He'd left his mother in a house where his wife had been taken, his children were in some sort of a trance and the attic was now a giant throat with rattlesnakes in it.

He suddenly realised that he needed to go home rather than on some wild goose chase so he could talk to a crazy old man. He began looking for the next place he could turn around.

He saw a dirt road just ahead on the left and as he nosed the SUV into it, he felt the icy chill sweep through his body.

The old street sign was still visible. It was Old Mesa Road. At least what was left of it.

He let the vehicle idle as he looked at the untended road that extended out into the darkness. Craig could see a couple of hundred yards ahead but beyond that, a low ground fog seemed to have settled onto the pitted and rutty landscape ahead of him. His headlights illuminated a broom snakeweed that had developed into a sizeable tumbleweed that slowly passed in front of him.

Craig had intended to turn around and head home but decided he'd come that far, he might as well confirm what he already knew which was that the road was going to end in about a mile. He eased the Explorer along the worn and potholed macadam until he came to the fog. It was rarely seen in the high desert but it did occasionally occur. The city reservoir wasn't that far away so Craig assumed that was the cause. As he entered the grey mass he was only able to see about ten feet in front of him and the road was getting rougher. The desert winds and hundred-degree temperature swings between winter and summer had taken a toll on the man-made surface. He seemed to be spending most of the time driving on packed earth. The dark grey remains of the macadam were becoming a rarity.

He finally came upon the first ROAD CLOSED sign. It advised that he had one hundred yards to go. He passed another sign more before reaching the last one. Its message was perfectly clear. ROAD ENDS. NO VEHICLES BEYOND THIS POINT.

Well, Craig reasoned, he'd tried. He was about to turn around when that little voice that used to get him in trouble as a child told him to keep going. The old man said he lived at the end of the road but, where Craig had stopped wasn't the real end of the road. That was three miles further on. He had only gone as far as where the road had been washed away many years ago.

He edged the SUV forward but only at walking speed. He knew where the flood had gouged away the land to a depth of over ten feet. It was coming up soon. The fog seemed to have thickened making it even harder for Craig to gauge exactly where he was. He recognised a giant boulder on his left that had somehow ended up there during the last ice age. It had been unofficially named Messy Rock by the locals partially as a play on the name Mesa, but also because the area around it was always a mess. People had thought the area around the boulder was a suitable location to dump their litter. It also used to be a place where kids would come out and climb and mess around but since the flood and the closure, they'd had to find somewhere a little more safe.

The boulder was on the very edge of the precipice of the flood channel. It hung precariously over the ten-foot drop almost as if it was willing itself not to fall.

Craig stopped the car alongside the huge rock. He could still see some of the graffiti the kids had sprayed years ago. They were all adults now, worried about work, money and maybe even their own children.

Craig felt a little disorientated. Though he was right next to Messy Rock, he could clearly see that the road continued ahead of him. He realised that there had to have been another rock that he'd never noticed because if it had been Messy Rock, his vehicle should have been mere feet from the drop.

He got out and approached the monolith. He turned on his Maglite and walked around to the back side. He shone the light halfway up the boulder and illuminated a small ledge. Craig remembered the day he'd sat up there with Jenny. She'd been feeling really down about her work prospects and couldn't seem to clear her mind. He'd had the idea of bringing her out here. So long as the kids weren't crawling all over the thing, Craig had felt it was a tranquil place to chill out.

Craig stepped closer and kept his light on the ledge. Even after what had to be eleven years, he could still clearly make out their initials that he'd carved into the stone.

That meant it was Messy Rock. It also meant that the road did not continue. Craig walked to the front of the Explorer and stepped very cautiously forward. After about fifty feet, he realised that the washed out road must have, over time, filled back in. The deputy had obviously not bothered to check out the road at all. He got back in the SUV and drove slowly forward. The road continued. It was all hard-packed dirt at that point. The paved part, at least what was left of it, had ended at Messy Rock even before the flood. But Craig couldn't understand how the road could exist at all. After ten years of non-use and zero maintenance how could it even be passable?

The weirdest thing was that the road seemed to offer a better ride than the rutted paved part before the rock. Craig kept driving though he still wasn't sure why. There was nothing out there but brush and snakes.

After a couple of miles, the dirt road took a turn to the right. As Craig followed its path the fog suddenly intensified to where he couldn't even see the front of the SUV. He opened his door and stared down at the dirt as he inched along.

The Explorer then died. The lights, the engine, the heater – everything just conked out. Craig got out and turned on his Maglite. Nothing happened. He proceeded to do what all technically savvy men do and shook it but it still didn't work.

He was stranded in complete and utter darkness coupled with the densest fog he'd ever seen. He fumbled around the centre console and found his phone. He felt for the home button then pushed it. Just like with the flashlight, nothing happened. For some reason everything electrical had stopped working. He was dying to check if his lithium-powered watch was still going but it was too dark to see.

As he sat alone in the middle of nowhere he began to fear that he was going to lose it. He wasn't feeling the crippling anxiety or having a bout of the chills – he was having something far worse. Hallucinations.

He was hearing things.

More specifically, he was hearing music. One moment it sounded obscure and distant, the next, it sounded a little clearer. It was Native American flute music. Its usual calming sound was having an entirely different effect on Craig. Miles from anywhere in complete blackness, the melody sounded eerily invasive. As he continued to listen to it, he thought he could see something out in the night. As his eyes grew accustomed to the darkness and the fog thinned slightly, he could make out a yellowish glow a few hundred yards away.

He got out of the SUV and stood in the dark for a moment. The light seemed to be coming from further down the old road. As his eyes continued to adjust, he found that he had just enough light to walk towards it. He wasn't crazy about abandoning his vehicle in the middle of the road but he was pretty sure it wasn't likely to cause too much traffic disruption way out there.

He started walking. The light grew stronger and the music more hypnotic. Craig realised that he could suddenly see the entire desert and the surrounding hills spread out before him. Though there was still no moon, the starfield was extraordinary. Their light was unobscured and gave everything a pale blue wash. They were so bright that they almost appeared to be in 3D. He felt he could actually see the dimensional depth of the galaxy laid out above him.

As Craig neared the yellow light he saw that it was coming from a storm lantern hung outside a simple one-room shack. When he was only a few feet away, the door opened framing Ahote in the glow from a fire burning in a small hearth.

"For you to have come, I have to assume that she has been taken," he stated.

Craig felt tears start to well up in his eyes. Being able to talk to someone who understood about what had really happened was a relief beyond words.

"And something's happened to my children. They're like zombies."

"Come inside. We have a lot to discuss," Ahote said.

He stepped aside and let Craig enter. Once in, he cast a quick eye out into the night then, satisfied, closed the door.

CHAPTER
EIGHTEEN

The inside of the shack was warm and surprisingly comfortable. Candles were dotted around the room, giving the space a golden hue. There wasn't much furniture and there was no sign of a bed which puzzled Craig considering the shack only consisted of the one room. Where did the old man sleep? The walls were adorned with dramatic paintings of eagles in flight. They looked old and original. A hand-carved wooden flute sat on the mantelpiece next to an old-looking transistor radio. Two large armchairs were situated facing each other in front of the fire. By its light, Craig could see that Ahote seemed to look younger. Ahote gestured for Craig to sit.

"Tell me what happened?" Ahote asked.

"What do you mean what happened? You knew all along that she was going to be taken," Craig shouted. "Where the hell is she?"

Ahote took a moment to answer.

"She has gone. By now Beyath has taken her life force. I am sorry."

Craig felt like he'd been hit in the stomach with a sledgehammer.

"What do you mean gone?" he asked in almost a whisper. "Gone where?"

"Your wife's mortal being would not have survived after Beyath took what she needed. Her body would have been consumed during Beyath's transition back to the fifth realm."

"I don't understand what you are saying."

"I am saying that Jennifer is no longer with the living in this timeline."

"Please stop talking in spiritual gibberish," Craig said as he lowered his head to his hands. "I just need to know what is going on, in simple English."

"There is nothing simple about what has transpired, nor about how it can be rectified," Ahote advised.

"Rectified?" Craig raised his head. "We can bring her back?"

"No."

"Then what the hell are you…"

"You and I will have to stop Beyath from ever existing in this time," Ahote stated. "That is the only way to ensure that your wife will not be taken."

"You're doing it again," Craig pleaded. "Please just tell me what you are talking about in a way I can understand."

"I will tell you everything you wish to know but I must warn you, once you know these things, you will never view this world in the same way again."

"I'll take that chance."

"I am what is referred to as a shaman," Ahote began. "You would have heard it called a medicine man. I was a spiritual guide for my people. However, I was different from the others. I was born with an ability to move within the timeline of my own life."

"Are you trying to tell me that you can time travel?"

"No. There is no such thing as time travel. What I am able to do is simply revisit a time that I have already lived in."

"I'm not sure I see the difference." Craig sounded very sceptical.

"There is a huge difference. I have already lived in – let's say 1996. I existed then and left pieces of my spirit in that moment. I am simply able to step through the folds of time into my earlier existence."

Craig was staring at him with his mouth wide open.

"Simply?"

"I can see that you doubt what I am saying," Ahote said.

"Does that surprise you?" Craig replied.

"No. Not at all. But what may surprise you, Mr Edmonds, is that we are both at this moment in 1996." Ahote smiled.

Craig started to get to his feet. "Thanks. I can see that I'm wasting my time here."

"Where are you going?"

"Home," Craig said.

"You have no home here in 1996. You are still in Arizona living with your adoptive mother."

"I don't know what you're up to, but I think it's best for your own safety to stay as far away from me as possible," Craig said angrily.

"When you arrived and passed through the fog, your sheriff's vehicle ceased to work. Your flashlight and phone also did not function. The reason was simply that the technology that powered those things has not yet been invented. Even the batteries are incompatible with the time."

"What about your Jeep?" Craig asked.

"It is a 1994 Jeep Cherokee. It can work today because we are in its time. The reason it works in 2021 is simply that it has been carefully cared for and any electrical repairs have been made with parts from the mid-1990s. Let me show you something a little simpler."

Ahote picked up the radio from the mantelpiece and handed it to Craig.

"Please, turn it on. I'm afraid there is limited reception out here especially in 1996, but you may want to try 94.1," Ahote suggested.

Craig took the radio and turned the power/volume knob. The tiny shack filled with the sound of static. Craig turned the tuning dial to 94.1. Pink Floyd's 'Comfortably Numb' was just coming up to Gilmore's amazing solo.

"So, what am I supposed to get from this? A radio station that plays Pink Floyd. Wow. That is a miracle."

"Please, just listen."

Craig reluctantly listened to the guitar solo. As it ended, a DJ's voice took over.

"Amazing solo. One of my favourites. You are listening to Planet Radio on 94.1, your best choice for rock in Southern Utah. It's coming up to the hour so let's go over to Jake in the newsroom."

"*Despite agreeing to stop their testing of nuclear weapons in the Mururoa Atoll, France has detonated yet another device. It has been three years since their last test in 1993 and leaders from around the world have condemned France for this latest test. President Clinton has already spoken to French President Jacques Chirac to lodge a formal complaint. In other news…"*

Craig turned the radio off. "It's a cute trick but I'm not buying it."

Ahote shook his head at Craig's stubborn determination to not believe him.

"Put your coat on – we're going for a little drive."

Craig followed him out to his Jeep. He noticed that the fog had completely vanished. Ahote drove away from his shack along the road that Craig had used earlier that night. After a few hundred yards Craig asked him to stop.

"Can you put your lights to full beam, please?"

Ahote did so.

"Is something the matter?" he asked.

"I left my Explorer out here. It's gone," Craig said.

"Of course it's gone. It won't be built for another twenty-three years."

"I don't know what you're up to, but stealing a city vehicle is a serious offence."

"Give me five minutes. Then if you still feel like it, you can talk to me about the severity of stealing cars."

Craig glared at him but didn't say anything. Ahote took that to be as good an acceptance of the terms as he was likely to get.

They kept driving. After a few minutes, they saw Messy Rock just up ahead.

"Stop here," Craig commanded. "I can put an end to this right now."

Ahote stopped alongside the boulder. Craig got out.

"Come with me. I have something to show you."

Ahote started to get out of the Jeep.

"We need a flashlight," Craig said.

The old man reached into the glove compartment and retrieved a large yellow emergency flashlight then followed Craig to the back side of the rock.

"Shine it up there." Craig pointed to where he knew the ledge would be.

The beam from the light wasn't as strong as the LED he'd used earlier but it did the job. The ledge was clearly visible.

"Look on the right side of the ledge about two feet above it."

Ahote looked but could see nothing but rock.

"There is nothing there."

Craig took the flashlight and scrambled up the boulder. He reached the ledge and shone the light directly at the spot where he had carved his and Jenny's initials. They weren't there. Craig sat staring down at Ahote.

"You won't even be meeting her for ten years."

"Enough of this shit. I have to get home."

"Not yet. You gave me five minutes. Please, get back in the car," he insisted.

Ahote drove until they reached 89A then turned right heading towards Kanab. Craig never said a word. He just sat staring angrily out of the passenger window.

As they approached the town, Craig pointed to the right side of the road where a used car and RV sales lot was closed for the night. It was full of pickup trucks, large SUVs and every sized RV trailer one could imagine.

Craig had never seen it before.

"What the hell is that place?" Craig asked.

"That's Kanab Auto Sales. They have some good deals."

"When did they open up? I come down this road twenty times a day and it's never been there before."

"You are asking the wrong question. You should ask, when did they go out of business? That would better explain why you have never seen them," Ahote replied.

Craig gave him a confused look.

"They went out of business two years before you arrived here."

Craig was about to reply but they had reached the town proper. He felt the chills start to creep up from the base of his spine. What he was looking at was not possible. On the right should have been the new BLM centre, the La Quinta Inn, then a few blocks further down, the Hampton Inn. All had been built in the last few years. Except they weren't there.

On the other side of the street should have been Wild Thymes Café, but instead there was only the old building that housed the Three Bears ice-cream parlour. It was obviously still in business but closed for the night. They cruised past Glazier's, the town's other supermarket. It looked exactly the same, then again it had always looked like something from the fifties.

"Turn in there," Craig ordered, pointing to Glazier's parking lot.

Ahote turned left into the empty lot. Craig jumped out of the Jeep and ran to the store windows which were plastered with print ads showing the weekly specials. The chills increased as he neared the building. Something was very wrong. It had been a long time since sirloin steak could be had for $1.79 a pound. He looked at the pages of impossible deals. He then looked at the top of one of the ads. It read – GLAZIER PRICE BREAKERS FOR JANUARY. Craig looked at the top of the print ad and saw the date. January 19, 1996.

Craig felt his legs turn to jelly. His Camp Pendleton therapist had always warned him that the symptoms could return. He'd never mentioned hallucinations but hell – here they were.

Ahote looked down at Craig with an expression of concern and empathy.

"I know that it is hard for you to grasp that what you are seeing is real. You are now in my timeline and I chose to recall this particular date. It is not an illusion or a hallucination. You are in 1996. This is Kanab in January of that year."

Craig looked up at him with a mixture of fear and disbelief.

"Why are we here?"

"Let me first explain what it is that I do," Ahote began as he sat next to Craig. "When I found out that I had the power to go back to times I had lived in, I realised that such powers are only given with an expectation of using them to benefit others. Coupled with my shaman training and skills, I had the ability to rectify certain evils that had already occurred."

"So, you can get Jenny back?"

"Please, let me finish so that you understand what can and cannot be done. First of all, I am not capable of making any physical changes within my timeline. However, I discovered that others who I chose to accompany me, can affect change. Most humans only exist on one plane. A single dimension driven by the laws of the sciences. What isn't understood is that invisibly interwoven within this plane are others that are not governed by such restrictions. In these dimensions, the laws of physics can be bent or even broken. These alternate planes of existence are supposed to remain separated from ours, but over time fractures have formed that have allowed incursions from one dimension to another."

Ahote studied Craig's expression to make sure he was following his words.

Craig nodded weakly back at him.

"Go on. I'm listening."

"Beyath is a witch. She was born in England in the seventeenth century. It is said that she found the lost writings of Morgana after the death of Arthur."

"Arthur?" Craig asked.

"King Arthur," Ahote stated matter-of-factly. "I am not saying that I believe in the Arthurian mythology, only that it is part of the legend of Beyath. She was able to increase her powers beyond the first dimension. While the other witches were being rounded up and drowned or burned into extinction, Beyath hid in plain sight within the fifth realm. She found that she could extend her life by a quarter century each time she consumed the life force, or soul as you would call it, of one of her own bloodline. This has been her existence for almost 400 years."

"What does she do between those times?" Craig asked.

"She simply exists. She has become pure evil. Most of the time she doesn't even take human form. She feeds on suffering and pain. If she can't find it naturally, she will create it herself."

"I still don't see what Jenny has to do with any of this. Why did this Beyath person choose my wife and what the hell's wrong with my children?"

"As I told you when we first met, it's all there in your wife's family history," Ahote said. "As for your children, they are in a transcendental state. Most likely Beyath placed them in that condition so they wouldn't interfere with her taking their mother. They will come out of it on their own."

"Why didn't she just kill them if she is so evil?"

"Because one of them may provide her with the life force she will need twenty-five years from now," Ahote explained. "What did you find of your wife's history?"

"We looked online but it just seemed like an ordinary family tree," Craig insisted. "There were a few relatives that did seem to have disappeared."

"A search on an Internet ancestry site can only tell you so much. You would have been lucky if they had produced ancestry going back a few hundred years. Jenny's history can actually be traced back to the twelfth century. She was a direct descendant of Beyath on the English side of the family. When Beyath was young she bore three children. That was before she found the writings and devoted herself to mastery of the dark arts. The first life force she took was from one of her own offspring."

"She killed her own child?" Craig asked. "That's beyond dark."

"That describes her well. She has taken and killed a member of her bloodline once every twenty-five years."

"Her aunt went missing in England twenty-five years ago," Craig stated.

"I know," Ahote replied. "In January of 1996 to be precise."

Craig's expression changed as he gawked at Ahote.

"We're gonna try and stop her, aren't we?" Craig asked with a mix of awe and disbelief.

"No. You are going to try and stop her. As I said, I cannot affect change. I can, however, get you to where you need to be which is in the village of Hambleden, forty miles west of London. We will be flying tonight from Los Angeles. Gina Winslow, Jenny's aunt, disappears from her cottage in three days' time and we will lose one and a half of those days in travel."

"What am I supposed to do? Rescue Gina?"

"No. You are going to kill Beyath before she can take her."

They drove out of the parking lot and were about to head back to the shack.

"I want to see our home," Craig suddenly announced.

"It's not your home. It won't be for many years," Ahote replied.

"I don't care. I want to see it."

Ahote sighed as he signalled a left turn onto HWY 89 heading east. A short time later they turned onto Johnson Canyon Road then stopped at the dirt drive that led up to the house. It was still very early in the morning and no lights were on inside the dwelling.

"Drive up," Craig said.

"That would not be a good idea. The owner is elderly and very willing to protect his property. He keeps a loaded shotgun by the front door."

"How do you know these things?" Craig asked.

Ahote simply shrugged.

"I'll walk. Keep the engine on, just in case."

Craig got out of the Jeep and started up the drive. He had grabbed Ahote's flashlight and was using it with his hand partially covering the lens. It gave him just enough light to avoid the mini ravines where water had washed away the hard-packed soil.

He reached the top of the drive and could see the dark outline of the house against the star lit sky. He had hoped that seeing their home would give him some sense of comfort or feeling of belonging but it did neither. As Ahote had said, it wasn't yet their home. Craig let a small beam of light illuminate the side of the house. It wasn't the cheerful canary yellow they'd painted it. It was the drab weather-worn reddish/brown that had taken them almost a month to scrape off before replacing it with gallons of Moonlit Yellow.

Craig was about to head back down the drive when a light went on in what he knew to be the master bedroom. He quickened his pace. He was halfway down the drive when he heard the front door slam open. Craig ran the rest of the way.

They didn't speak until they were back on HWY 89 headed for Kanab.

"Was that worth it?" Ahote asked.

"Shut up," Craig replied.

Ahote smiled to himself.

CHAPTER
NINETEEN

The two men sat by the fire and talked until the first light of dawn. Ahote explained that the only time that Beyath was mortal was when she emerged from the fifth realm in human form. She still had powers but could not escape death if her body was destroyed outside of the portal. He warned Craig that while that offered a brief opportunity, Beyath would do everything in her power to not be harmed. He further stressed that the real extent of her powers was not known but that myths referred to them as limitless.

"And you think I can kill her?" Craig sounded unconvinced.

"You have certain skills that we are going to put to good use," Ahote replied.

"You think my being a deputy sheriff is enough to subdue a 400-year-old witch?"

Ahote smiled. "No. I do, however, think that one of the Marine Corp's best snipers might be up to the task."

Craig felt the light-headedness he'd felt just before the worst days of his PTSD. He had avoided any conscious thoughts about his days as a sniper for over twelve years. They were like a healed wound. The skin might have sealed over, but if you picked at it enough it could still bleed causing the healing process to have to start all over again.

"I can't," Craig stated.

"You can and you must. I am not asking you to kill an unknown woman or child. I am asking you to kill the creature that took your wife."

Craig closed his eyes and focused on what Ahote had just said. He knew it was the only way that he would see Jenny again. He reopened his eyes and looked over at the other man.

"What do I do about her powers?" Craig asked.

"You will be over 500 yards away on a hill that overlooks the cottage."

"What about Jenny's aunt? Are we going to get her out of the house?"

"No. She will have to remain in the cottage as she normally would if we were not involved," Ahote explained.

"Isn't that a little dangerous?" Craig asked.

"It's the way it has to be. Beyath can see through the portal. She would know if Miss Winslow wasn't present. She would not risk the transformation to being mortal unless she knew that her target was there."

"Can't we just destroy the portal before she comes through?"

"No one knows the exact relationship between her and the portal. If it is destroyed before she becomes mortal she could remain in her inhuman form until she can find another entry point. Legend states that she can use any reflective surface once she has empowered it."

"Why does it have to be reflective?" Craig asked.

"It is believed that the reflection is able to hold the memory of her form before and after the transition. It is from that memory that her abstract energy is able to recreate itself."

"Then why not destroy it when she has become mortal? If the mirror is gone she can't go back," Craig suggested.

"There are a number of reasons," Ahote replied. "Firstly, when she is in mortal form the mirror becomes almost indestructible. It can only be damaged once she has passed back through and the portal is resealed, which at that point is too late to do any good. The other issue is that her powers are so great that no one knows the extent of the damage that she could cause if trapped on our side of the portal."

"How does she manipulate the mirror? Is there a switch or control mechanism?"

"Supposedly, there is a word that activates it, but though I have found many references to it, I have been unable to find mention of what the word actually is. When Beyath has used the oral key to turn the mirror from its solid state back into a form that she can pass through, she has never left anyone behind who has heard the word."

Craig gave Ahote a long stare.

"You do realise how crazy this all sounds?"

"Unfortunately," Ahote replied, "it does not sound crazy to me at all. I have spent countless years investigating just this type of creature. What's amazing to me is that so many of these evil entities have been described in early writings and depictions in stone and paint. Horror movies have been made based on myths about these very creatures in the belief that they were purely fictional. Very few people have thought to ask why, if these creatures are simply the result of fantasy or delusion, there are so many of them described with almost identical characteristics and powers throughout history in every single part of the globe."

Craig looked to Ahote to answer his own question. Ahote just stared back.

"You're not expecting me to answer that, are you? You're the expert on this. I'm still not convinced that I haven't had a complete psychotic break and am right now in a padded room somewhere in a VA hospital."

"You have not had a mental break. Your mind is healthy, but you are predisposed to disregard the irregular and only follow the facts. We see a shadow pass through a room at night and we immediately look for the rational answer. A car headlight outside, or a curtain moving in a breeze. The possibility that an entity has momentarily entered your universe never occurs to you," Ahote advised.

"Damn right. If I thought creatures were wafting in and out of other dimensions every time I saw something move out of the corner of my eye I'd go crazy," Craig declared.

"Then you are not going to enjoy the next few days, my friend."

"Just so long as I get Jenny back, I can put up with a little weirdness."

"That is my hope." Ahote smiled.

"When are we leaving for LA?"

"We are booked on a flight at 10:30 am from St George to Los Angeles. It should take an hour and a half at which point we'll have some time to kill before our TWA flight to London."

"TWA? They don't exist any more," Craig said.

Ahote gave him a long, disappointed look until Craig realised what he'd said.

"Got it. They haven't gone bust yet. Can we stop in town so I can get some money out of the ATM?"

Ahote shook his head. "You are having trouble with adapting to the timeline, aren't you?"

"Hey, I'm still gonna need money in LA and England," Craig replied defensively.

"Using an ATM card that hasn't been issued yet, trying to withdraw money you don't have from an account you have yet to create?"

"I guess I see your point."

Ahote reached down beside his chair and produced a worn soft-sided briefcase. He reached inside and brought out a clear plastic folder. He tossed it over to Craig.

"In there you will find a credit card in your name, an ATM card, UK pounds and US dollars. Your pin for both cards is your home address street number."

"That's not very safe," Craig observed.

"By the time it actually is your home, that bank will no longer exist," Ahote said flatly. "You will also find a current 1996 driver's licence and passport. Your watch has not yet been produced so you can buy something at LAX. I took the liberty of purchasing you some timeless pieces of clothing from Dukes in Kanab. I got you a piece of cheap hand luggage as well."

"I get the distinct feeling that all of this required some serious planning."

"You appear to be catching on. Finally!"

"I have another question that I just know will piss you off," Craig said.

"I can't wait."

"What about my mom and kids? They're in the house waiting for me, twenty-five years from now. Is there a way I can get a message to Julie that I'll be gone for a few days?"

"When you return, it will be the same day that Jenny was taken, but she won't yet have been taken. She and the children will greet you as they always do when you return home from work. Your mother will still be in Arizona because you haven't called her to come and help. So, as you can see, there is nothing more that you have to do."

"Except fly six thousand miles, shoot a witch before she steals a dead woman's soul, then fly back again and return to my present day."

"Exactly," Ahote smiled. "I knew you'd understand eventually."

"I just realised something. I'm gonna need a rifle in the UK."

"We are being met by a friend when we land in London. He has managed to… borrow a prototype of the latest sniper rifle that will be used by the British Military. I believe it's a modified version of the Arctic Warfare's Magnum rifle. Its designation is L115A3. It's accurate to one point two kilometres. You will of course have time to familiarise yourself with the weapon in the grounds of the house in which we'll be staying."

"I know that rifle well. It might be brand new on this day of your timeline, but it was considered old hat when I was in sniper training in Virginia."

"Good point," Ahote said. "Any more immediate questions?"

"That's about everything from me for the time being," Craig announced. "Any chance of grabbing some breakfast in St George before the flight? When I was in the Marines, I always used to get really hungry before a mission."

"I'll see what I can do Gunnery Sergeant," Ahote replied.

"Outstanding, sir!"

CHAPTER
TWENTY

They left Kanab in the dark. An hour later, dawn was just starting to slowly open the shutters on a dazzlingly clear day as they wound their way into the town of Hurricane. By the time they reached the Wagon Wheel Diner in St George, the first rays of winter sunshine were casting elongated shadows across the red hills.

Craig was feeling both nauseous and hungry at the same time. He was excited about the mission but was also tormented over why it was needed. Even though he knew it was 1996 and that he and Jenny hadn't even met yet, driving away from Kanab had felt like an act of cowardice.

"Are you able to cross over into the other dimensions?" Craig asked as he worked to get a wedge of pancakes securely speared on his fork.

"No. And I wouldn't want to," Ahote replied between bites of his huevos rancheros. "The other dimensions are not places for mortals such as us. There is no mirror dimension that scientists believe exists. They are nothing like ours at all. Imagine a place where the laws of physics don't apply in any way."

"I can't," Craig answered.

"Exactly. That is why no human being could ever survive the transition, let alone the conditions within one of the alternate planes."

"If you can't pass into the other dimensions, then how are you able to fight what comes out of them?"

"As you just said," Ahote replied. "They have to come into this existence. The dimensions are filled with any number of entities that live solely to harm and destroy. Thankfully almost all remain in their own realms. I only become involved when one has strayed into ours."

"Beyath doesn't exactly stray into our dimension, does she?" Craig asked.

"No. She does not. Then again she was not conceived in the fifth realm. She chose to cross over in order to save herself. Because of her powers, she found a way to survive the transition."

"Why do you sometimes call it the fifth realm?" Craig asked. "Is it the same thing as an alternate dimension?"

"Yes. I should attempt to stick with the same lexicon while you are learning. The fifth realm is part of Hopi mythology. It is the plane where true evil resides," Ahote said.

"So, your people knew of the dimensions as well?"

"This is what I was trying to explain earlier. Mankind used to be much more aware of the darker side of existence. Then, through science, religion, even schooling, we were taught to not believe, therefore we no longer see. Have you ever heard of an artist named Hieronymus Bosch?"

"I've heard of the detective, Hieronymus Bosch," Craig replied.

"He is a fictitious character in books and TV. The artist was real and lived in the fifteenth century. He is known for his depictions of hell and ultimate evil. He was considered insane at the time. The fact is, we believe that he was able to see the other dimensions and simply painted what appeared to him. You should google him when we get back."

"One more question," Craig announced. "When you travel back in your timeline, can you place a bet?"

"Why is that the one question that always gets asked?" Ahote sounded disappointed.

"Probably because it's everyone's time-travel fantasy except maybe going back and killing Hitler," Craig replied.

"As I have already explained, I am not able to make changes in my timeline. Making a bet would be considered a change."

"How could winning some money possibly change anything?" Craig asked.

"Okay. Let's say I know the results of a horse race and I place a huge wager on it to win. By placing that bet, the odds change and when the horse does win, everyone gets less of a payout. Now you ask, so what? No big deal. What difference did my betting on the horse really make? A man that also bet on the horse takes home $5,000 instead of $10,000 because of the lower odds. Had I not interfered and he had received the bigger amount, he would have been able to buy the nicer, sportier, faster car that he'd had his eyes on. He would have ended up smashing the car into a tree and dying in the accident. He would never go on to fulfil his original destiny which was to become a serial killer preying on young dark-haired women that remind him of his ex-wife. By not winning as much, he has to settle for a far more mundane, slower car. It's not sporty and has poor acceleration and the man never loses control of it and thus, he never perishes in an accident. Ten women ultimately die horrific deaths by his hands. All because I placed one bet on a horse I knew would win. I hope that gives you the sense of how a seemingly harmless action can have dire consequences."

"You are one gloomy person." Craig tried to eat a mouthful of pancakes but could suddenly only taste raw flour.

Ahote shrugged and attacked his eggs.

The men finished their breakfast in silence.

They turned back onto the 15 freeway then turned off at St George Avenue. Craig looked baffled.

"Where are we going?"

"The airport."

"You're going the wrong way," Craig advised. "You should have stayed on the 15 till the 7."

Ahote gave Craig one of his despairing looks.

"What?" Craig asked.

"We are not going to the airport that was only built in 2011. I thought it best that we go to the one that's actually in operation now."

"Don't get snarky."

"I'm not getting… snarky. I am just a little surprised that you seem to still be having trouble with the concept of time," Ahote said.

"I wasn't having any trouble with the concept of time before you arrived. Time just slowly passed in a pleasing linear fashion. Then you enter my life and I'm back to 1996. Of course I'm having trouble with it. You may want to consider asking your next sidekick if they would mind doing some time travel before just making it happen."

Ahote drove in silence for a moment.

"I apologise," Ahote conceded. "You are absolutely right."

Ahote pulled the car into an open-air parking lot.

"What are you doing?" Craig asked.

"We're here."

They checked in at the SkyWest desk within the tiny terminal then waited in the equally small departure lounge. Craig was amused to see that the only attempt at a concession stand or gift store was a single vending machine. It offered a selection of individual pieces of fruit on the first two levels, questionable-looking sandwiches on the third and Hostess Cupcakes, Twinkies and Snowballs on the fourth level.

They watched their SkyWest Embraer turbo land and deplane less than a dozen people. Half an hour later the same woman who had checked them in announced that boarding was now starting.

The flight took just under an hour and a half. As they started their descent into Los Angeles International Airport, Craig looked down at the vastness of the city. He'd only been there once before and hadn't liked it. It didn't seem to have a soul. It was just a vast spread of concrete roads and drab stucco buildings.

They had hours to kill until their TWA flight to London so decided to walk to the Tom Bradley terminal and check out the various shops outside the secure departure zone. Ahote needed to buy their hosts in the UK various requested items. He also confessed to having a sudden craving for some dark chocolate Toblerone.

They tried both gift stores in the terminal but couldn't find it. At the second shop, the manager was so intrigued by Ahote's failed search that she produced the Toblerone confection catalogue. They looked at it together. There was no such thing as dark chocolate Toblerone.

Craig turned to Ahote with a satisfied look.

"I've got to tell you, I'm quite surprised that you are having so much trouble with timelines. I mean, spending twenty minutes looking for a chocolate that won't be made for another ten years. I'm disappointed. That's all I can say."

"You can be an ass sometimes, Mr Edmonds," Ahote said as he headed back to one of the gift stores, presumably to buy something made in that era.

Craig had to smile.

As the two went through security, Craig was amazed how different it was from his experiences of modern air travel. There were no long lines of people waiting to have their carry-on X-rayed and then have themselves scanned and even swabbed for explosives. All they had to do in that era was have their tickets checked then walk through a metal detector.

Instead of sitting in the crowded departure lounge, Ahote led Craig up a set of unmarked stairs to the mezzanine level that housed the private lounges for each airline. Ahote walked into the TWA reception area and showed his ticket as well as a gold card with the TWA logo embossed on the front. They were shown into what looked to Craig like a five-star hotel lounge. At one end, a self-serve bar displayed a vast selection of top brand spirits as well as expensive wines and beers. All free. Craig wondered what would have happened in his drinking days had he ever found himself with such unlimited options. At the other end of the lounge was a buffet table with an amazing-looking display of gourmet finger foods. Smoked salmon, French cheeses, pâté – you name it, it was there.

Craig was stunned to see Ahote stop first at the bar and pour himself a few fingers of Heradura Silver tequila. When he joined Craig at the buffet he could see Craig glance down at his glass.

"I thought somehow that you were a little more zen?"

"I hate flying. I need this just to get on the plane," Ahote advised.

"You don't have to give me an excuse. I might have a problem, but that shouldn't stop anyone else having a drink. Especially if you're scared."

Ahote glared at him as he knocked back the tequila. Craig could smell the alcohol and for a moment felt the beginnings of the craving. He cleared his mind and focused on the selection of food until the reflex had passed.

Craig had done his share of flying in military transport as well as commercial aircraft when he was in the Marines. He was very used to sitting at the back of the plane while children screamed for attention as their parents drank away the hours in a futile attempt to dull the noise coming from those same children.

His first clue that their flight was going to be different was when the lounge receptionist announced that pre-boarding had started for their flight and that they were welcome to board at any time. He was used to being in the last group called after all overhead storage was taken and he had to crawl over people to get to his centre seat in a block of five.

When the military books commercial, you get the seats nobody else wants.

When they got to the end of the jet bridge and stepped into the 747 fuselage, Craig started to turn to the right as was the norm for him. Ahote stopped him and a flight attendant directed them to the very front compartment.

Craig had never been in first class in his life. He took one look at the giant reclining seats with enough legroom for an NBA player and decided that he was going to like it. He asked Ahote how he could afford what had to be very expensive tickets.

"The people who support what I do are very generous," he answered.

The ten-hour flight passed quickly. While waiting for dinner to be served, Craig turned to Ahote who was reading a Steven King book with an illustration of a drain and a paper boat on the cover.

"When exactly did you first discover that you could go back into your timeline?" Craig asked in a subdued tone.

Ahote made a big deal out of folding a page over to mark his place. Craig had a momentary flash of the time he had done that to a book in front of Jenny when they were first dating. She had not been pleased about his treatment of someone else's hard work and had let Craig know it.

"I was seven years old," Ahote began. "I was sitting in front of a campfire with my family when my grandmother reached to retrieve a piece of meat from the flames. She somehow got her jacket sleeve too close to the flames and it caught on fire. The coat had been treated with bear fat to repel rain. The fat ignited and she was engulfed before anyone could do anything. I remember screaming hysterically then suddenly felt as if I was falling. The next thing I knew, I was sitting at the same campfire with my grandmother telling the same story. I somehow knew that I had gone back a few minutes in time. I saw her start to reach for the meat and stopped her. I retrieved it for her. She never caught fire and lived another twenty years."

"And after that you could go back whenever you wanted?" Craig asked.

"Not at all. I didn't even recognise that I had gone back. I thought it was a trick of the mind or something. It wasn't until a similar situation when my brother fell through the ice and I again stepped back a few minutes and thus prevented it that I understood that I had the gift."

"That sounds like you were aware of people going back before it happened to you?"

"I had heard the tales of the time-walkers but thought it was just legend. Later I found that I was not unique and that people had been practising it since the very beginning."

"You mean there's other people who can do it?" Craig asked in amazement.

"I would guess one out of every million or so people have actually time-walked," Ahote said. "Many more have the ability but have yet to realise it."

"If that many people can do it, why isn't it better known? Something like that would be reported like crazy," Craig stated.

"It all goes back to our minds being trained to find the simpler explanation. Time-walking is very well known, however all but a very few of the practitioners simply call it déjà vu. They get a sensation they have been somewhere before and dismiss it as a trick of the mind, when in fact, they were actually there moments before in their own timeline."

Craig wanted to ask more but when Ahote opened his book back up and unfolded the page, he knew the conversation was over.

They ate a five-star restaurant-quality meal and then watched a first-run movie that Craig remembered going to see as a child. They both managed to sleep until their tray tables were being positioned in preparation for their hot breakfast before landing.

Craig had often wondered why first-class passengers always seemed to get off long-haul flights looking awake and refreshed, whereas the human cattle who had been trapped at the back of the plane stumbled off the aircraft with the dazed look of people who had just woken up in the drunk tank. Now he knew. The pampering, the fully reclining seat, the food and the toiletries all made a huge difference. He wondered if he and Jenny could find a way to one day fly first class together. He knew she'd love it, but she would never permit spending five times the amount to be on the same plane going to the same place as everyone else on the aircraft. She would consider it a complete waste of hard-earned money.

Just before landing, they both had to fill out local immigration cards. Ahote filled one out first then had Craig copy the UK address information onto his. They were also given a red 'Fast Track' card. Craig had no idea what it was until they reached Heathrow Airport's terminal 3 international arrivals hall. There was a queue of at least a thousand people waiting to go through passport control. Ahote gestured for Craig to follow him as they walked past the roped entry to the queue line and instead found a cordoned-off aisle at the far end of the hall with no line at all. They handed their red cards to an attendant then proceeded to a smiling immigration officer. Craig tried to get a look at Ahote's passport to see his real name but Ahote seemed prepared for such prying and managed to keep those details covered the entire time.

Once welcomed to the UK by the immigration official, they made their way through the green customs area then into the arrivals terminal. Ahote spotted a driver holding up a card with the words INTERNATIONAL DIMENSIONS printed on the front. The man may have been acting as a chauffeur but to Craig, he had ex-army written all over him. He was Craig's height but seemed wider. The extra width appeared to be pure muscle. His greyish blonde hair was cut to a uniform one-inch length.

The man took their carry-on and escorted them to the pick-up area just outside terminal 3 where a gleaming Jaguar Vanden Plas was waiting. It was parked where most cars would have been immediately moved on or, if left unattended, towed. Their car hadn't been touched. Craig made a mental note to ask Ahote about that.

They drove to the M4 then headed west. Craig had never been to the UK before and was amazed at how rural it seemed. Then again they were driving away from London and its immense urban sprawl. The driver joined the A404 until he got off onto the Henley road. After a few miles they turned onto an unmarked lane then immediately turned again and drove through a pair of electrically operated wrought-iron gates.

Craig looked out of the car window in wonder as they passed acres upon acres of manicured lawn surrounded by dense woodland. The remains of a recent snowfall were still present in areas where the winter sun couldn't quite reach and melt it away.

"This all belongs to a private house?" he whispered.

"All 500 acres," Ahote whispered back.

"This is nothing. The property in Scotland makes up most of an entire county," the driver added. Craig could clearly detect a Northern Irish accent.

After a further few minutes, Craig could finally see the main house. He had trouble taking it all in.

"Oh my god! It's Downton Abbey," Craig exclaimed.

"I've never heard that before," the driver replied.

"You wouldn't. It's a thing on American television," Ahote advised the driver.

"That won't be aired for another fifteen years," he whispered to Craig through gritted teeth.

The driver laughed.

"Don't feel too bad, Mr Edmonds. The first time I worked with Ahote we went back almost fifty years in his timeline. I put my foot in my mouth so many times I'm still amazed I could walk at all."

"You did a splendid job, Connor. I miss our little trips," Ahote said.

"It was either you or the wife. She won. Have you found a replacement partner in crime yet?"

"Not so far. I live in hope that the right person will magically appear one day."

They pulled up to the front portico just as an immaculately dressed man in his mid-thirties came out of the house and waved.

Craig felt his throat go dry.

Though he was casually dressed, what he was wearing was unquestionably expensive. The shoes alone looked like they cost at least a month's deputy sheriff salary.

He wasn't sure what the man did in 1996 but Craig knew that in ten years' time, Edward Jenkins would become the prime minister of the UK.

CHAPTER
TWENTY-ONE

Edward greeted Ahote like a long-lost friend. Craig was introduced but found himself completely tongue-tied.

"Are you all right?" Jenkins asked.

"My guess is that he recognises the future you," Ahote suggested.

"I'm not the PM yet so there's no need for any special treatment," he said.

Craig looked up at the palatial mansion then back at Edward.

"If it helps, this isn't my house. I would hardly end up as a Labour PM if I had this sort of money. This might even be too much extravagance for a Tory to get elected," Edward explained.

"This house is owned by one of our sponsors. As he rarely uses it, we are lucky enough to be able to take advantage of its privacy and size," Ahote explained. "Edward here is a junior cabinet minister at the moment and is able to help us navigate through difficult situations, should the need arrive."

"Does that mean that the government knows about the different dimensions?" Craig asked.

"God, no," Edward laughed. "Most of them have the same belief system as a dog. If they can't fuck it, fight it or piss on it, they don't believe in it."

"But you believe, don't you?" Craig stated.

"As this is obviously going to become a lengthy conversation why don't we get in out of the cold and have some coffee?"

Edward led them through a massive entry hall that was bigger than Craig's entire house. The walls were covered with what he assumed were family portraits dating back hundreds of years. All the people in the paintings looked dour. There wasn't a smile to be seen. They all seemed to have the same dark-rimmed eyes that appeared to be looking at you no matter where you stood in the space.

"Creepy, isn't it?" Edward asked. "They jokingly call this the viewing gallery. They call it that because everyone who walks through here feels like they are being watched."

Edward showed them into a large but comfortable morning room that was tucked away at the back of the house. Craig hadn't realised that they were on a hill, but could see through the double French doors that the back garden sloped gently down to what appeared to be a stream in the distance.

"Wow," Craig said. "Does that stream belong to the house?"

"Actually, that's the River Thames. The banks are part of the property. The river itself can never be privately owned… fortunately."

Connor appeared and placed a silver tray with a large cafetière, four sturdy-looking mugs and an assortment of English biscuits onto a finely inlaid wooden coffee table. Craig was surprised when he then sat down to join in the conversation. For some reason he had presumed that Connor was more house staff than guest. He realised that his thinking was also based entirely on *Downton Abbey* hierarchy.

"You asked me outside whether I believe," Edward said. "I never considered it until Ahote here turned up on my doorstep one evening. I was a barrister at the time and was part of a task force that had been formed after a series of brutal child murders had taken place throughout Northern England over a three-year period. The police were stymied, the country was terrified and the media was demanding blood."

"Terrible time," Ahote stated.

"Anyway, this gentleman appeared before me and had a tale to tell. He seemed to believe that a creature from an adjoining dimension had found a way to slip back and forth between ours and the one in which it lived."

"And you believed him?" Craig asked.

"Not for a second." Edward shook his head. "I asked him to please leave and not to bother me again. He agreed but told me that if I needed to talk to him I would be able to find him at an address he gave me in Yorkshire. He said that I was to go to the very end of the road."

"That sounds familiar." Craig looked over at Ahote.

"Anyway, a few days later a young boy who was playing in a park on the outskirts of Newcastle, not fifty metres from his parents, was horrifically slaughtered and disembowelled. The parents couldn't be sure but they thought they saw something just before the attack that resembled the creature from the *Alien* movies. Obviously, that lead wasn't given much credence by the police, however, it struck a chord with me especially after what Ahote had told me. I looked up the address he'd left with me and was surprised to see that it was in the middle of the Yorkshire moors. The address couldn't have been accurate as the road at that point became no more than a desolate path before it petered out into inhospitable marshlands. For some reason I drove up there and followed his instructions to the end of that road. I had to walk the last quarter mile in a dense fog as my car had completely conked out. I found Ahote living in an old shack."

Craig turned and stared at Ahote with renewed awe.

"I found that I had gone back into Ahote's timeline. It was eleven years earlier," Justin continued. "We went up north to where Ahote told me the first child would be taken. I wasn't even aware of that first child's murder. This was years before we even knew that we had a serial killer. Ahote had given me a shotgun and told me exactly where to stand. I saw the young boy as he ran past the old remains of a rock wall. Suddenly a creature rose behind him. It didn't really look like the alien. It was, however, not of our world or even within our conscious ability to describe something so completely impossible. Thankfully, it wasn't aware of me. It was only focused on the young boy that it was stalking. Just as it reached out to grab him, I stepped forward and fired both barrels. The thing screamed and as we watched, it seemed to change shape then dissolve into the air around it."

"That was it going back to its own dimension," Ahote added.

"Did you kill it?" Craig asked.

"I don't know," Edward admitted. "What I can say is that when we returned to present day, at least present day back then, there was no task force because there had been no series of child murders."

"That's amazing," Craig said.

"It was amazing. It opened my eyes to a reality that I never knew existed. Or if I did, it was completely subconscious and I chose to ignore it. Ever since then I have been part of a group that monitors potential dimensional incursions. We are well funded and Ahote is our secret weapon."

Craig stared down at his coffee mug.

"Is there a problem?" Edward asked.

"Go ahead, Craig," Ahote smiled. "I believe I know what you want to ask."

Craig looked uncomfortable but continued anyway.

"Is Ahote the only person you have that can take people back to destroy one of these creatures?"

Edwards nodded solemnly. "Unfortunately, he is."

"What happens when Ahote gets too old to continue the work?" Craig asked. He looked over at Ahote with an apologetic shrug.

"That is a big question for all of us and one we are scared to even contemplate," Edward admitted.

Ahote stood and walked to the French doors that led to the back patio.

"I have considered this at great length as my timeline gets closer to its end. I believe that, before I become infirm, it may be possible for me to go back to my younger years and basically live my life over again. The problem is I don't know for certain what that could do. My current real time is 2021. The question is how long am I actually permitted to spend in the past. The longest period that I have ever remained out of real time was seven days. When I returned to my present day, no time had passed at all. Can I really expect to live an entire life again while my real timeline never moves beyond the moment I stepped back? It's a nice thought, but that would then bring up the obvious question of whether I would still be able to move back freely within, what is in effect, a second timeline. If so, would that not make me capable of achieving some form of immortality? I somehow doubt that I was granted that level of power. In any case, none of that will be of any help to you at all in a future present day where I no longer exist."

The room remained quiet as they contemplated the unanswerable questions that Ahote had raised.

Finally, Connor broke the silence.

"Maybe it's time to show you to your rooms and Craig, there's a special present waiting in yours."

"If I am in the same room as last time, I know my way," Ahote said. "Connor, why don't you show Craig to his?"

"You do have the same room though it's been modernised since you were last in it," Connor smiled.

Connor took Craig up a mahogany staircase that led off the main entry hall. There were more paintings of seemingly unhappy family members adorning the walls but thankfully they seemed to not have eyes that tracked your every movement.

They reached the first landing and headed down a long corridor with heavy damask-lined walls and small crystal chandeliers every twenty feet or so.

Connor stopped in front of a pair of heavy oak doors and swung them open. Craig almost gasped. His room was huge and overlooked the sloping back gardens. A king-sized canopy bed rested against one wall. At the far end of the room, a fire was burning within an inglenook fireplace. Despite the grandeur of the room it had a comfortable and cosy feel to it.

The only thing that detracted slightly from the room's aesthetic charm was a sniper rifle and sound suppressor lying in an open case on top of the bed. A box of .338 Lapua Magnum ammo sat next to it.

Craig's reaction on seeing the weapon was mixed. He felt something akin to the joy of seeing an old friend while at the same time felt the dizziness that preceded the chills. He told himself that what he was there for was not to murder an unsuspecting enemy combatant in cold blood. His assignment was to kill a confirmed monster seconds before it murdered an innocent woman in her home.

"It's going to work out," Connor said. "I know what you've been through but this is completely different. What you'll be doing tomorrow will save not just your wife's life, but countless more that would have been preyed upon in the future."

Craig took a deep breath then slowly nodded his head.

"I'll have to practise. I haven't shot a rifle, especially that one, for a while." He gestured to the bed.

"Hardly anyone has," Connor commented. "It's brand new. You'll recognise the Schmidt and Bender scope though. That hasn't changed."

"Don't forget, it's not brand new to me," Craig replied. "I've used it on three missions. What range will I be working with? I know it's good for over a kilometre."

"Less than half that. The challenge won't be the distance. It'll be lighting and position. You'll be on a hill, shooting downwards at about a thirty-five-degree angle through a glass door, into a cottage sitting room."

"What type of glazing?" Craig asked.

"Single, so that's one plus," Connor said.

"No chance of the door being left open?" Craig suggested.

"Not in January in England. That would be an immediate red flag."

"Can we at least make sure the lights are left on in the room?"

"They will be," Connor nodded.

"Does the woman know what's going to happen?" Craig asked.

"No. We're going to sedate her but keep her off to one side in the sitting room. We will also have a spotter close to the house and a clean-up crew ready to dispose of the body."

"What if things go wrong? Will anyone else be armed in the house in case we need help?" Craig asked.

"No. The witch would put anyone close enough to shoot her into a trance before they could fire. We're counting on you. I suggest you try not to screw up."

"Thanks for the advice," Craig replied ignoring the jibe.

Connor left him to freshen up before lunch. Craig took the time to check out the rifle. He'd always liked everything about it. The weight and balance were perfect. Holding it somehow just felt right and in some strange way made him feel complete. His actions as a sniper played a big part in causing the stress that had almost destroyed him, however Craig recognised that it was also a part of what had made him who he was.

He checked the cheap swatch he'd bought at LAX and saw that it was getting close to the time he was supposed to join the others. He quickly washed his face and brushed his teeth before heading downstairs. He realised that he should probably have changed clothes after eighteen hours of travel but decided that could wait.

When he reached the entry hall he heard voices from the morning room where they'd had coffee. He detoured and walked away from the sounds to do a quick exploration of the house. He found a magnificent living room that was bigger than the entire ground floor of their yellow house. All the paintings and furniture were covered with white dust sheets. Craig thought that the room looked as if it was haunted by a child's notion of a ghost.

He walked through to the next room and found a formal dining room with a table the length of an Olympic swimming pool. Again, everything was enshrouded in white linen. Next, he found a door which led him to a darkened corridor. He walked part of the way down and saw double doors on his right that opened onto a massive ballroom. There was no furniture in the room whatsoever but three chandeliers, each the size of an SUV, were suspended from a twenty-foot-high Louis XIV-style ceiling. These, too, were wrapped in white.

Craig decided he'd done enough touring and retraced his steps back to the main entry hall. Seeing the emptiness of the once grand entertaining spaces made him feel a certain hollowness inside. The way the white sheeting was covering everything so that the rooms could quickly return to the glory days of masked balls and seated dinners for a hundred, was, to Craig, a depressing show of hope. Craig had already learned that the owner rarely visited the grand house. Its glory days were in the past.

As he entered the morning room, he saw that they were gathered around an old CRT television. It seemed so archaic compared to the flat screens he was used to. They were watching a BBC news report. A family of five had died in a freak house fire just west of the town of Twyford. Images on the screen showed the charred remains of a small, detached home.

Ahote turned to Craig.

"Beyath has arrived."

CHAPTER
TWENTY-TWO

After lunch Connor drove Ahote and Craig to Hambleden to do a site visit on Gina Winslow's cottage and its surroundings. They drove along the narrow Wargrave Road until they reached the historic town of Henley-on-Thames. Connor turned onto the Marlow Road then continued until they reached a beautifully restored mill that sat nestled among trees on the banks of the Thames. He turned left up an extremely narrow road that was signposted to Hambleden.

As they entered the tiny village, Craig had a strange sensation of already knowing the place.

"I feel like I've seen this village before," he said.

"Do you watch *Inspector Morse*?" Connor asked.

"Yes. Jenny and I love it."

"Then you have seen Hambleden countless times."

"That's a shame. I thought I was having a psychic episode."

"No, just remembering a TV episode," Ahote joked.

They drove past the Norman church then turned left down a narrow lane, quaintly named Pheasant's Hill Frieth.

After a few hundred yards, they turned right up a steep drive until they stopped at a dead end. They left the car and Connor led the two across a wooden stile then walked further up the hill. There were still patches of snow on the ground despite the winter sunshine. Craig couldn't help but notice how beautiful and serene the area was. They hiked for no more than five minutes then stopped at the edge of a dense wood.

He pointed down the hill to a white cottage with cheerful green shutters. A wisp of smoke rose from its chimney. Bits of snow still clung to the slate roofing.

It looked like a Christmas card.

Craig removed the rifle scope from his pocket and looked down at his target. Connor had been pretty close with his distance estimate. Craig knew that the 500-yard distance would not be a factor. The downward trajectory, however, could be a problem because of the angle the bullet would travel through the glass panes within the door. In daylight, it was almost impossible to see into the room, but Craig estimated that if Beyath was more than ten feet from the door, he wouldn't get a clean headshot and if she was further than fifteen feet from it, he wouldn't even get a bead on her torso.

"Can I get any closer?" Craig asked.

"Depends on the weather tomorrow," Connor replied. "If it's a clear night, you'll be pretty bloody visible if you go further down the hill. Up here against the background of the trees you'll be a ghost."

"I don't like the angle. At best I'll only have a clear target as long as Beyath stays within fifteen feet from the glass door."

"You're forgetting how cramped those old cottages are. The sitting room is only eleven feet wide. Your bigger issue will be the horizontal radius. Your viewing arc is only going to be about thirty to thirty-five degrees."

"That's tight. She'd better stay within that area. Wouldn't it be easier if I approach the door from the garden with a silenced handgun? There'd be little chance of missing from that range," Craig suggested.

"That goes both ways," Ahote advised. "She would sense you before you saw her. It's not worth the risk. Besides, the mirror is on the wall right in the centre of your arc. You just need to shoot her the moment she materialises."

"Oh, is that all?" he replied sarcastically.

Ahote just shrugged his shoulders.

"How dark will it be when I'm supposed to do this?"

"Gina will be home from her shopping in Henley at around six. She will be tranquilised as she walks from her car. She will start feeling sleepy in fifteen minutes and will be out cold fifteen minutes after that," Connor explained. "By that time, it will be pitch-dark."

"How are you giving her a delayed tranque?" Craig asked.

"Topical application. One of our team will shake her hand when she gets out of the car saying they're glad to see her. Being British she'll take the hand despite not having a clue who the person is."

"And why do you think Beyath will wait thirty minutes before making an appearance?" Craig asked.

"We don't," Ahote answered. "We're assuming that she will wait until Gina is in the same room as the portal before grabbing her. Less distance and less fuss. When Gina gets home she will first spend time in the kitchen putting her shopping away. That's where she'll begin to feel sleepy. Hopefully, she then will do what she does on most afternoons anyway and have a little nap in her armchair in the sitting room."

"There's a lot of supposition that goes along with this, isn't there?" Craig commented.

"Yes, there is. By trying to assassinate a 400-year-old witch from the fifth dimension, we are basically doing the impossible anyway so there are bound to be quite a few variables," Ahote replied.

"How do we know that Beyath will choose that time to take Gina?"

"Her dimensional spirit arrived in the house yesterday. We know that through the actions of the local wildlife," Ahote explained. "Just like at your house, Gina's attic is now full of a menagerie of psychotic vermin. We also know that her transition takes roughly forty-eight hours. That means that she will have the ability to transition by midday tomorrow. Gina being out of the house is the only reason Beyath won't transition earlier. She is very weak at the end of her twenty-five-year cycle. She will want to transition as soon as she can once Gina is in the house then grab her immediately while she has the strength."

"Ahote, if this goes sideways, are you able to go back again to the same point so that we would have a second chance?" Craig asked.

"I don't know. I never have. It's a very good question but I would prefer not to have to test it out. I do know however, that I am unable to go further back while I am already back in my timeline."

"How do you know?"

"I tried once. Nothing happened," Ahote said.

"What would happen if we burned down the house while her life force is in it?"

"All that would accomplish is leaving poor Miss Winslow homeless. Until Beyath has transitioned to human form she could still re-enter her dimension at any time," Ahote explained.

"If she's that weak and had to go back to her dimension, wouldn't that be the end of it? I mean, she wouldn't be able to find another way through, would she?"

"This is not an exact science. We would all prefer to end the problem tomorrow," Ahote declared.

"Then we really need to get this right," Craig said. He tried to sound cavalier, but knew that his and Jenny's entire future depended on his actions the next day, to say nothing of poor Gina. If anything went wrong and Beyath somehow survived, they would not. He wasn't sure he could face returning to a time when Jenny no longer existed.

"When can I start practising with the rifle?"

"It'll be dark by the time we get back. There's a night scope you could use, otherwise you'll have to wait till tomorrow. You've got most of the day to practise," Connor said.

"I won't need the night scope for the mission if I'm shooting into a lit room. I'd prefer to practise in daylight so tomorrow will be fine. Do we know what the weather's supposed to do?"

"This is the UK. We've rarely got the faintest idea of what the bloody weather's going to do," Connor smiled.

Few words were exchanged on the drive back. As they pulled through the gates and wound their way up to the main house, Craig could see by the beams of the Jag's headlights that it was beginning to snow. It was light and at the point when the flakes had yet to organise themselves and fall in one direction.

He thought of Tim and Sally back at their house. He wondered if they were still in their trancelike state. He had to remind himself that in reality, if that was the right term, they hadn't even been born yet, at least not from where he was in Ahote's timeline. He hoped that Ahote had been right when he said that their time wasn't progressing while he was here, on mission. He had no idea what they were thinking, or had been thinking when he last saw them, but he hoped to God that their young brains hadn't been tortured or shocked by what they had gone through.

He wanted things back the way they were.

CHAPTER
TWENTY-THREE

The first thing Craig noticed when he woke up the following morning was the quiet. It was as if he were wearing industrial ear protectors. He walked to the window and pulled open the curtains. The world outside was white. Everything had been blanketed by snow. It was beautiful. It could also be a real problem for their mission.

Craig threw on a pair of sweats and headed downstairs. The others were in the kitchen drinking coffee.

"What does this do to us?" Craig asked.

"I've got a white combat suit being delivered within the hour. Obviously your black camo won't work with all this shite on the ground," Connor stated, "You'll be lying on cold snow for quite a while, so that's gonna be interesting. The snow suit is insulated but still…"

"The biggest problem is going to be with Miss Winslow and her shopping trip," Edward advised. "She's a tough old bird and will go out in almost any weather, but not when the streets are impassable."

"The main road to Henley is closed?" Craig asked.

"No, that's been ploughed. It's the road up to Hambleden and then the lane up to her cottage that are untouched," Edward said.

"Why is that a problem?" Craig asked.

The others stared at him as if he were simple.

"Don't look at me like that. What about all these resources you are all supposed to have? Bring in a plough and clear the road and her street. Seems pretty obvious to me."

Edward gave him a surprised look.

"Amazingly that solution never entered our minds. We were just discussing the possibility of having her evacuated for a suspected gas leak or something."

"I think you'll find that having the roads ploughed would be a damn sight easier and a whole lot less conspicuous," Craig said.

"Well done, Craig," Ahote smiled. "Sometimes it's the simple solutions that are missed."

Edward turned to Connor.

"Get a plough up there, will you? Tell them to clear the whole village to make it look authentic. Also, have it stay up there in case there's additional snow later."

Connor nodded and left the room.

"Any concerns about shooting in snow?" Edward asked.

"Having never done it other than in training, I'd have to say no. The only slight hiccup will be the light from the room reflecting back onto the snow. It's not a huge deal but having nothing but black except the light in the house was ideal. But don't worry. I'll make it work."

"Good." Edward nodded. "So, what's first on the agenda today?"

"Practising," Craig stated flatly. "Where can I do that?"

"Right there on the hill." Edward gestured towards the back gardens. "The lawn, which is somewhere under the snow, stretches out for almost a thousand metres so you've got plenty of space to mark out your distance."

"That's not a problem. Do you have anything I can use as a target?" Craig asked.

"I think something can be arranged. I'll have Connor meet you out back in ten minutes. Sound good?" Edward asked.

"Sounds perfect."

When Craig stepped out onto the snow-covered patio ten minutes later, he was stunned to see six life-sized, rubber, range-training mannequins posed in sitting positions on the patio wall.

"I was told you needed some targets," Connor grinned. "I hope these will do?"

"You just happened to have these lying around?" Craig asked.

"Doesn't everybody? I should warn you, they're bloody heavy."

"Can you give me a hand getting them down range?" Craig asked.

"That's why I'm here."

Connor hadn't been joking when he said they were

heavy. They were meant for emergency re-enactments and were intentionally weighted to make them appear and feel more like real victims. After pacing out 500 yards, Craig made a line in the snow where the dummies needed to go. The two then manhandled each one down the slippery hill until all six were lying side by side on the hill.

Connor then ran back up to the house and returned with six-foot-long rebars that each ended in a sharp point. The rubber mannequins had Velcro attachment points on their back which were easy to affix around the metal rods. Forty-five minutes later, all six dummies were standing up in a line facing upslope towards the house.

While they were assembling the targets, it gave the two a chance to talk. Craig learned that Connor seemed to know everything about him already.

"So, what about you?" Craig asked. "What did you do to get noticed by International Dimensions?"

"A bit of this and a bit of that," Connor replied.

"I assume you were pretty good at the this and that?" Craig asked.

"I did what I was told and came back in one piece so if that qualifies as good, then yeah, I'm good," Connor answered.

"You're not gonna give much away, are you?"

"Wouldn't make much sense to do so at this point, would it? I mean, you're not one of us, are you? You're here because it's personal. Now, if one day you end up joining the team, I might just tell you a bit more about myself. Then again, I might not."

"Join the team as what?" Craig asked.

"Ahote needs someone to help him," Connor stated.

"Help him how?"

"How do you think? Doing the same thing you're gonna do later today. He has to have someone to do the wet work. He can't ever be the one to change the past. That has to be done by whoever goes with him into his timeline."

"That used to be you. Didn't it?" Craig asked.

"That much you already know, so there's no harm in admitting it," Connor said.

"I know you won't give me any details but can you tell me what it was like?"

Connor gave Craig a long, hard look.

"Sure. I'll tell you. I have never ever been so fucking scared and at the same time exhilarated in all my life."

"On which mission?"

"On every bloody mission. You're lucky that you're starting off with one that's actually human, at least part of the time. It's when you come across one of the buggers from another dimension that's managed to slip through. Your brain can't handle what you're even seeing. They're not like movie monsters. They're beyond the scope of even the best horror writers. Some have no real form at all. They're the worst. A wispy mass of sentient evil. Those ones can get into your head. No, you're lucky you're starting with this one."

"Are you saying she's not that dangerous?" Craig asked.

"I'm definitely not saying that. Any creature that has found a way to move between the dimensions has got to have some unholy powers. Thankfully, the witch has to take human form when she's in our world. Couple of shots from that rifle should finish her off nicely. Just don't bloody miss. You don't want to piss her off."

"With the exception of Beyath, why do these things bother to come into our dimension just to kill a few people?" Craig asked.

"Why do people pay a fortune to travel to Africa just so they can shoot some poor defenceless animal?" Connor replied.

"Are you saying they come here just to hunt?"

"That's my belief."

"That's horrible," Craig said.

"You're not here for tea and crumpet. You're here because it is bloody horrific."

"In that case, I'd better get to work," Craig said.

They walked back up to the patio. Craig already knew that everything was working smoothly with the rifle. He'd broken it down before going to bed. It was cleaned and oiled. The only wild card was his own ability. It had been a very long time since he'd used a sniper rifle. Connor had left an old blanket that he could use to lie on to save him freezing on the snow. He threw it down on the spot he'd marked out as his perch.

Connor went inside so as to let Craig practise in peace. He knew that his type were loners. They liked to kill in complete solitude. They didn't consider what they did to be a spectator sport.

Craig checked the magazine, banged it at few times against his palm then inserted it into the rifle. He stepped onto the snow-covered lawn and lay down as he would have to do later that day. He chambered the first round then sighted the mannequin on the far right. There was nothing but him and the target. All noise stopped, everything in his peripheral vision blurred and became of no consequence. He no longer felt the cold as he slowly breathed out. The dummy's head filled the scope. Craig held the crosshairs just above the bridge of the mannequin's nose.

Craig eased the trigger towards him.

Even though he wasn't using the sound suppressor for the practice, the sound of the rifle firing was muted by the layer of snow over the ground and the surrounding trees. Craig saw a black hole appear just above the dummy's right eye. He was about to adjust the scope when something caught his attention. A trickle of blood began to run from the wound. Craig was momentarily taken aback but suddenly realised what was happening.

Craig then heard laughter from behind him. He turned and saw that Connor had snuck out to watch Craig take his first shot.

"You're an asshole," Craig called back to him. "What did you use?"

"A tin of tomato soup. I think it was Tesco's," Connor replied with a grin.

Craig shook his head as he made a miniscule adjustment to the scope, then chambered another round. Sneaking a container of something that looks like blood into targets was an old sniper's prank during training. It had been done before to Craig and he'd always laughed it off. This time he'd been caught unaware. It brought back images that he didn't want to see. Especially not now.

Craig took aim at the same dummy and fired three shots one after the other. All three were within centimetres of each other directly above the bridge of the nose.

Connor nodded his approval at the other man's skill. He stepped back into the house. Jenkins and Ahote were sitting in the morning room drinking tea.

"How's he doing?" Edward asked.

"Good. The man can shoot."

"Any problems after seeing the blood, or should I say soup?" Ahote asked.

"If there were, he's got a good handle on it. I think he's gonna be fine," Connor stated.

"Do you think he knew it was a test?" Edward asked.

"No, I think he just thought it was a prank and that I was being an arsehole."

"Why do you think that?"

"Because he called me an arsehole," Connor replied.

"Good. We want him on his best game tonight," Jenkins said. "Do you think he might work with us after this?"

Jenkins looked hopefully at Ahote.

"I think that will be very dependent on how well everything goes later today. If he doesn't stop Beyath and his wife never returns, I doubt Mr Edmonds will be of any use to anyone."

"That would be a shame," Edward commented.

"Yes, it would," agreed Ahote. "A great shame indeed."

CHAPTER
TWENTY-FOUR

There was a team meeting in the kitchen at 1 pm or 1300hrs as everyone else was calling it. There were a lot of new faces in the room. Edward first advised everyone that the snow ploughs had been successful and that all roads were clear. He then introduced each person and outlined their responsibility for the mission. He advised that one member of the team was already active on site and couldn't attend the meeting. She was an operative who had made herself up to look like a middle-aged woman shopper. She was charged with ensuring that Gina didn't leave Henley too early. At the table was an older couple who would be responsible for shaking Gina's hand when she returned from Henley so that the topical tranquiliser could be applied. A young outdoorsy-looking couple was going to ensure that Craig wasn't disturbed on the hillside above the cottage. A young man who looked like he'd stepped right out of a Royal Marines recruitment poster would hover outside the cottage and act as spotter. If it was deemed necessary, he could enter the house and 'interact' with Beyath should Craig not succeed, though everyone hoped that such a risky option wouldn't be required. He was only to be used as a last-ditch measure. Lastly, three dour-looking men sat away from the others paying little attention to the specifics being discussed. They were the clean-up crew whose task it would be to ensure that all evidence of the encounter within the house was eradicated.

The team members went over their tasks in detail and confirmed all aspects of their mission. By 14:30, the meeting disbanded and everyone went their own way.

Ahote, Edward, Connor and Craig remained to discuss a few final items. One of them was a complete surprise to Craig.

Ahote had to somehow be in position within the house so that, once Beyath was dead, he could perform the traditional Kachina ceremony to ward off any remaining spirit presence from *Buaka*, the Hopi word for a night walker or witch. Ahote apparently performed the ceremony after every successful mission and had made it an irrevocable part of his participation.

Ahote was able to make himself undetectable to Beyath through the use of ancient shamanic meditation. He would remain in a self-induced transcendental state until he was needed. He felt that the best approach would be for him to enter the kitchen area once Gina had gone to sleep in the living room so he could be close when the time came for him to perform the ritual.

It was also decided that Craig shouldn't walk up to the woods behind Gina's house in his new white snow camouflage suit as it could attract attention and would be hard to explain. The rifle and the snow suit would therefore be put in place ahead of time by his protective detail. They would also ensure that nobody else got near it.

With nothing else to discuss, Edward bade them good luck and watched as Connor drove them off the property. He would have loved to be on site as an active player, but could not do so as it could undoubtedly jeopardise his standing in the government. He had to settle with managing the operation from a distance via radio communications.

They reached Hambleden just as the church bells pealed 16:00. All team members were equipped with US Secret Service-type communicators. One by one, each checked in and gave a brief sitrep on the hour. They advised that everyone was already in position or would be within minutes. The update from the Henley team member was good. Gina had been successfully waylaid and had unknowingly had tea with her 'minder' after discovering that she was an ardent collector of vintage Royal Doulton character jugs. Gina had been collecting them for years so was delighted to have a chance to talk to a fellow connoisseur. She was of course nothing of the kind. She had seen her collection when she'd carried out a recon visit to her home weeks earlier and decided to learn all there was to know about the disturbingly ugly pieces of porcelain in order to play her part.

Craig and Ahote were dropped off in the centre of the village and made their way separately to their appointed positions. Craig took the long way around to get to the woods behind Gina's cottage. In the forty-five minutes it took him, the last of the wintery daylight passed to the west being replaced by a brief twilight that was all too rapidly followed by complete darkness. The sky was overcast so there was no ambient light. This would help to ensure that Craig would be nearly impossible to see as he lay prone on top of the blanket of snow.

Craig retrieved the rifle from where his minders had left it. He removed it from its soft travel bag and gave it a quick check. He remained in the impenetrable shadows of the wooded area until the 17:00 sitrep. Everyone was in place except Gina herself. She was in a queue inside the Waitrose supermarket. The Henley team expected her to arrive back at her cottage on schedule at 18:00.

Craig put on his white Arctic coveralls and stepped out onto the snow-covered hill. He was taken aback by the sound his footfall was making. In the short time since the sun had set, the temperature had dropped and the surface of the snow had refrozen into an icy skim. To Craig, each footstep sounded like he was walking on a field of Rice Krispies.

He reached the spot he had chosen the previous day and lay down on the white surface. He found out, much to his annoyance, that the camouflage suit was made from a material that slid easily on icy snow. He couldn't imagine how that little fault was overlooked by the manufacturers and the procurement people. He had to move very cautiously to be able to get into a prone position facing down the hill. The last thing he wanted was to start sliding down towards the cottage.

At three minutes to six, the couple tasked with the topical transfer of the tranquiliser advised that Gina had returned and that they had carried out the application. There had been an unexpected problem when they saw her get out of her car and realised that she was wearing leather gloves. They had been forced to wait in the shadows until she had removed the gloves to retrieve her door key from her handbag.

They greeted her as planned, but she was so startled when the two appeared out of nowhere, that the handshake became a fumbling affair resulting in a much shorter contact period than they hoped for.

From his perch 500 yards up the hill, Craig saw lights turn on within the cottage.

He settled into his firing position and focused all his attention into the scope. His view into the house was unobstructed and clear. The inside lights gave him an almost perfect view of the mirror. It looked a lot like the one they had received in Utah. After about twenty minutes he could see Gina enter the sitting room. She was yawning. She passed out of Craig's view but was seen by the spotter from a different window as she sat in her favourite armchair. Minutes later, the spotter advised that she had fallen asleep.

Craig announced that he was shutting off his com unit. He didn't want any sudden distractions while shooting. He stared through the scope as he forced his heart rate and breathing to slow. Now was the hardest part of his job. The waiting. Craig focused entirely on the surface of the mirror. Any disturbance in its reflective quality would indicate that Beyath was coming through the portal.

Craig had no sense of time and was unable to check his watch without taking himself out of 'the zone'. He guesstimated that at least an hour had passed when he saw the first tiny ripple spread across the mirrored surface. It was so slight and so quick that Craig wondered if his mind was playing tricks on him. Then it shimmered again. This time it was more visible and lasted longer.

Craig breathed out as he rested his index finger within the trigger guard. He felt the cold metal against his bare skin. Despite the freezing temperature, he couldn't wear gloves. His touch against the trigger had to be felt by every single nerve ending. There was almost a sensuality of touch between him and the tiny strip of steel. The gentleness of his finger's pressure as he squeezed it towards him was as intimate as it was deadly.

If Craig had kept his com unit on he would have heard the commotion going on just outside the cottage. The external team member was desperately trying to let everyone know that Gina had somehow woken up. Obviously the hastily applied tranquiliser hadn't completely worked.

There was confusion about exactly what to do. She was starting to get to her feet.

"Everyone calm down," Edward's authoritative voice rang out in everyone's earpiece. "There is nothing we can do at this point. Keep your positions and stick to the plan."

Craig watched in awe as the surface of the mirror slowly turned opaque. The ripples on its surface became more organised and concentric. They moved away from the centre of the mirror in a circular pattern.

Something then blocked his view. Such was the suddenness of the interruption, he almost pulled his eye away from the scope. He realised that Gina had stepped into his sight. She was standing in front of the door staring out into the night. Over her shoulder, Craig could see the mirror surface becoming more agitated. Gina yawned and reached up to pull the drapes across the window. Ahote was suddenly behind her. He held his hand over her mouth and applied pressure to the vagus nerve on her neck. She went limp in his arms. Ahote stared directly at Craig as if knowing exactly where he was. He then gently lifted Gina over his shoulder and moved out of Craig's sight.

Craig again had a perfect view of the mirror. His blood ran cold when he saw that there were no ripples and that the mirror had lost its opaque sheen. He assumed that Beyath must have sensed Ahote and retreated back from her transitioning. Craig didn't know what to do. This had been his only chance to fix everything. Craig felt his heart pounding and his breathing quicken. He could feel the chills beginning to form at the base of his spine. He knew that he had to somehow get his emotions in check. There would be plenty of time to let himself sink into the dark pit of despair once it was confirmed that they had failed. The soldier that was still inside him knew that until that time, he was on duty and had to be alert and ready to complete his mission.

He focused on his breathing and brought his heart rate back under control. He stared through the scope with complete determination, even as he felt a single tear run down the side of his face.

"Come on, you bitch," he whispered. "Come out, come out, wherever you are."

Craig wiped away the moisture that had formed in his eyes then shut them tightly for a second while he willed himself into rigid focus.

He looked through the scope with the detachment that comes from years of cold-blooded killing.

A single circular ripple formed on the mirror as a wizened hand and arm slowly reached out through the surface and into their dimension.

CHAPTER
TWENTY-FIVE

Craig watched as the other arm appeared near the bottom of the mirror. The claw-like hand grabbed hold of the frame and began to pull. The head then started to emerge. Wispy white matted hair was plastered against it. Craig thought it looked like some grotesque birthing ritual. The rest of the body emerged out of the portal then just lay, unmoving, on the sitting room floor.

With agonising slowness, Beyath started to rise up on thin, shaky legs. She was so emaciated, Craig didn't understand how she could even be alive. She was also naked. Her skin, if you could still call it that, was almost black and looked to have the texture of burned paper just before it crumbled into ash. It was puckered where tendons pulled the muscles taut. Her bones almost protruded, stretching the ancient, weathered flesh to the point where it looked as if it could split open at any moment. Her breasts were no more than loose skin flaps that hung down from her chest.

Beyath then raised her head. The skin was so tightly pulled back against the skull that her blackened teeth were visible in a horrific rigor-like grimace. She brought her body up to its full height and took her first breath in their dimension. Beyath then opened her eyes. They were dark yellow but unnaturally bright. Her pupils were black pinpricks in the centre of her irises.

She looked around the room and spotted Gina, asleep in her armchair.

Craig had her head in the crosshairs and was ready to fire but the sight of that pathetic yet horrific creature momentarily caused him to hesitate. He pushed his mind to ignore what she looked like and just remember what she was. His finger started to apply pressure against the trigger.

Beyath stopped. She turned away from Gina and faced the window. She began to smell the air as her eyes darted in every direction. She looked feral. She took a shuffling step towards the window then skittered the rest of the way with an almost crablike motion. She was fast – very fast.

Her face filled Craig's rifle scope. He could see the witch's eyes scan the darkness for something. Then they locked onto Craig. He didn't move a muscle despite feeling suddenly very exposed. He knew she couldn't actually see him at that distance in those conditions but the eyes remained riveted on him. Her already terrifying grin stretched even wider revealing even more of her blackened fetid teeth.

Craig decided the time was right to end the nightmare. As he began to apply the needed pressure to the trigger, the image in his scope began to change. He was no longer looking at Beyath. He was looking at the face of his mother.

It wasn't Julie. Beyath had turned into his birth mother. She was wearing the same clothes she had been wearing when he'd last seen her before he went to bed that night in Apache Junction.

She smiled at him. It wasn't the smile that she used when she'd been drinking. It was the smile from a happier time when his father came home with flowers instead of the jug. He could see her beautiful hazel eyes as they stared back at him with a look of love and compassion.

Her lips began to move and Craig realised that he could hear her voice perfectly despite the glass door and the distance. It was as if she was in his head.

"Hi Craigie. How's my big boy?" she said. "Would you like me to make you a peanut butter and jelly sandwich for lunch?"

Craig found himself nodding. He removed his finger from the trigger guard and loosened his grip on the rifle. He was about to put it down when one of his minders appeared by his side.

"It's time to shoot, sir," the woman said.

"It's my mother," Craig replied.

"It's not your mother. Your target is trying to fool you."

Craig heard the words but couldn't understand quite what they meant. All he could see was his mother's face in the window. It was all he could care about at that moment.

Then Beyath made a mistake.

She transformed again. This time into his father. Craig was suddenly looking into the face of the man who'd been responsible for the destruction of his family. He didn't feel hate, but he didn't feel the overwhelming adoration he'd had for his mother.

He tightened his grip on the rifle and placed his finger back into the guard.

Craig watched as his father's lips started to move. He was about to speak as his mother had done. Craig knew that he would hear the words with complete clarity. The thing was, he didn't want to hear anything from the man who took away his mother. Initially with the jug, then finally with a bullet.

Craig pulled the trigger. The sound was still loud even with the suppressor but the snow stopped any reverberation or echo.

Beyath was impossibly quick. She tilted her head with such speed that Craig's shot missed. Beyath was no longer Craig's father. She had returned to her regular age-ravaged form. She skittered back towards the mirror and almost made it before Craig fired three shots in quick succession. He chose to not even attempt to aim for the head as it was flitting violently back and forth as she moved. He opted for centre mass. All three shots were on target. Beyath's anguished scream was so loud that the sound had actual form. Craig felt the wave hit him as she fell back through the portal.

Craig broke cover and ran down towards the cottage. His minders followed close behind. The other team members were already in the house when Craig reached it. They gathered in the sitting room to make certain that there was no further threat from Beyath. Gina was still out for the count in her armchair. A gentle smile rested on her lips.

Ahote signalled for everyone to follow him into the kitchen. He shut the door.

"As we know, things did not go exactly to plan," Ahote whispered. "The tranquiliser certainly didn't perform as expected. Here's what we do. Firstly, two of you remove the mirror and get it out to the van. Then come back and take the telly and the silver tea set from in here."

He pointed to a cupboard next to him.

"One of our uniformed officers will be here when Gina wakes up. He will inform her that she has, unfortunately, been burgled soon after being rendered unconscious. That will explain the improvisation I used when she woke up in the middle of the operation. We already have the replacement glass for the door. Let's get that installed immediately. The other task is that the clean-up team needs to check for bullet holes in the area around the frame. There's one obvious one where Craig missed but we have to make certain that none of the shells that hit the target passed through her. The rifle is in the sitting room. Someone please grab that as well. Everyone clear?"

They all nodded and left the room to carry out the various tasks.

"How are you doing?" Ahote asked Craig. "You look a little pale."

Craig shook his head. "That was very bizarre. Did you see her change from where you were?"

"She never changed at all. She just made you think she did. I knew there was something wrong when you hadn't taken the shot immediately while she was at the door."

"She became my mother. My real mother. I could hear her speaking to me." Craig took a deep, calming breath. "I couldn't shoot her."

"And yet you did," Ahote stated.

"Only because she overplayed her hand. She should have stayed as my mother but for some reason she turned into my father instead."

"She was looking for whichever instilled the deepest reaction," Ahote advised.

"I don't think she liked the reaction she got from turning into my father. I hit her three times. Centre mass."

"I saw that," Ahote said.

"You don't seem pleased," Craig commented.

"I am very pleased. I just prefer it when we have a dead body to destroy."

"She couldn't have lived after those three shots."

Ahote patted him on the back. "We should make ourselves scarce. Our work is done. Connor will be waiting in front of the church."

"By the way, that was quite a nifty move you made on Gina. I think I've only seen Mr Spock use that."

Ahote smiled.

"You know – from *Star Trek*," Craig added.

"I know it very well, Mr Edmonds. I have had the privilege of watching the very first airing of the original series a number of times." Ahote grinned as he led Craig out of the cottage.

"Wait," Craig said. "I shouldn't be wearing this anymore." He gestured to the white suit.

"Leave it here. The team will get rid of it."

Craig climbed out of the nylon overalls.

"One thing though," Craig began. "I hate that we're stealing things from that sweet lady. That doesn't really seem fair. I mean, I get the mirror, but her TV and tea set? That's really low."

"Once we're out of the way and the police, or rather our police, interview her, they will amazingly track down the burglars and return her goods to her tomorrow."

"Nice," Craig replied smiling. "What about your Kachina ritual?"

"I will conduct a very abbreviated version before we leave. I have no idea how long Gina will be out. I don't want her waking up to find an old Indian in her living room making strange gestures at the walls."

Edward was waiting for them at the front door of the mansion. "I hear it went well."

"There were a few hiccups as there often are," Ahote said. "But it does appear that Beyath should no longer be a factor."

"You're comfortable saying that when we don't have the body?" Edward asked.

"Nobody could have survived that shooting," Craig stated.

Edward looked to Ahote for confirmation.

"She was struck in the centre of her back with three shots. I agree with Craig. They had to be fatal."

"Could you tell if she was dead before re-entering the portal?"

"No," Ahote answered. "However, she was almost crippled by her need for Gina's life force. Even if by some miracle she had survived once she had transformed within the portal, she had only days left to live. This was her only chance for another extension to her horrible life. We stopped that."

"Where's the portal now?"

"The mirror would have been smashed as soon as they had it out of the house and inside the van," Connor advised. "The frame should be at the crematorium by now. It will soon be nothing but ash."

"Good," Edward said. "Why don't you get yourselves cleaned up and be back down here in thirty minutes. I am taking everyone out for a little celebration."

"I hope the celebration involves that Indian restaurant in Twyford?" Ahote smiled. "Gaylords, isn't it?"

"We have the whole place to ourselves," Edward grinned.

CHAPTER
TWENTY-SIX

Craig had never eaten Indian food before. He was overwhelmed by the colours and the foreign smells. Craig came from a background where Mexican food was about as exotic as it gets. Edward ordered for the table. Everyone but Craig was drinking Taj Mahal lager. At Edward's insistence, Craig tried a drink called a mango lassi. It was a blend of yogurt, spices and sweet pureed mango. He at first thought he would be craving a beer being surrounded by so many drinkers, but the lassi was so delicious he hardly missed the alcohol at all.

The waiters began bringing the various starters including spicy poppadum, onion bhajis and vegetable samosas. The various sauces were explained to Craig and he tried every one. The mains arrived in a flourish of more rich colours and scents. Craig was warned which were hot and which weren't. Being a devotee of hot Texas-style chilli and believing he was immune to spice 'heat', he ignored the warnings and tried a large forkful of lamb phall.

"That's not hot at all," he announced prematurely after his first bite. The others at the table watched with anticipation knowing that it takes a few moments for one of the hottest curries in the world to have an effect.

Craig had a second forkful halfway to his mouth when it hit him.

"Oh my god!" he cried as he tried fanning air into his mouth. He desperately reached for his water glass but Ahote stopped him.

"That will only make it worse. Eat the raita with some of the naan bread. That will cool your mouth down." Ahote pointed at the cucumber and yogurt dip and passed him half a piece of the Indian flat bread.

As soon as the burning feeling abated Craig began sensibly following the instructions of the other diners. It had been a long time since he'd felt the camaraderie of professionals after a big mission. It was also the first one he'd ever experienced stone cold sober.

They all shared stories of their exploits, some successful, some not. Some of the stories were about operations that had gone so bizarrely wrong that they were actually funny. It was hard for Craig to accept that the missions they were talking about were actually about operations where they were fighting real monsters. A few days earlier, he hadn't believed such a thing was even possible.

"How is it people don't know about this?" Craig asked at one point.

"People do know. People have always known," Edward explained. "Millions are reported missing every year around the world. Most are eventually found. Others can be traced to human predators, but that leaves tens of thousands per year that vanish without any trace and are never located."

"Then why isn't something being done?" Craig asked.

"It is. You are dining with part of the something," Connor reminded him.

"Is this it? Is this all we have to stop them?"

"Not at all," Edward answered. "We are just one team. However, because of Ahote and his ability to go back, we have become something of a specialised force. We don't just try to destroy the entity, we try to prevent the deaths before they even happen."

Craig ate a mouthful of chicken Madras while he let that sink in.

"You said the other teams fight the entities. How? They can't know exactly when an attack is going to happen."

"They stay in the present and follow the being into their dimension after the attack," Edward said.

Craig turned and shot Ahote an icy glare then looked back at Edward.

"You're kidding? People go into the other dimensions?"

"It's not something I'd kid about. The casualties are high when we go through but sometimes it's the only way to stop the entity. The insertion teams are the bravest of the brave and are willing to step into another reality to hunt down a killer."

Edward raised his glass without saying a word. The others all followed suit. Craig raised his as well. They all took a drink then resumed eating. The lightness of the earlier mood never completely returned.

The next morning Edward bade them farewell from the portico as they piled into the Jag.

"I hope we will see you again, Mr Edmonds. We could use the help."

Craig smiled and waved. He had no idea what to say. All he could think about was getting home to Jenny and the kids and leaving everything he'd heard about the darker side of our existence to people who were trained to deal with it. He was a deputy sheriff in a small town in Southern Utah. He was perfectly happy dealing with drunken tourists and petty theft. He had no wish to become a warrior against creatures from alternate dimensions. That was the stuff of Hollywood action movies. Craig preferred his enemies to be human and preferably from the same time he was living in.

Connor drove in silence along the M4 as they headed back to Heathrow Airport. He could feel a tension in the car as if he were expected to ask more questions or discuss what had happened the previous day. Craig preferred the tension to hearing any more about the supernatural. He couldn't fathom how these people did what they did every day and still were able to keep some semblance of sanity.

Craig suddenly had the urge to call Jenny from the airport to let her know that he was heading back home. He knew he couldn't. Jenny was still a child with fantasies about princesses and magic castles. The only monsters in her world were the imagined ones that lived in the darker areas under her bed or at the back of her closet.

The flight back was uneventful but long. They were travelling with the sun, so remained in daylight the whole way. Despite that, Craig managed to sleep for over half the flight. The sound of the engines was hardly audible in the first-class section and that coupled with his mental exhaustion over the past few days was enough to put him out like a light. As they approached LAX, Craig had to ask something that had been bothering him.

"Before we left for England, you told me that no human being could survive the transition from our dimension to one of the others. But Edward said that there were teams who did cross over to find the creatures that had attacked us."

"I did say that. I didn't feel you were ready for anything beyond the mission at hand. I knew once you'd killed Beyath you would better understand what Edward was saying last night," Ahote replied.

"So, we can cross over into other dimensions?"

"Yes and no. To do so requires extensive training and highly specialised protective wear. Imagine what astronauts go through then multiply it by ten."

"How did the first people who tried to cross know what to do?" Craig asked.

"By the time the first person crossed over, robotic probes had been doing it for over ten years."

"So, the first people to go over were properly prepared?"

"We thought so. We were wrong. Lots of brave people died during the first few years of human crossings," Ahote said.

"Is it safe now?"

"The crossing itself is relatively safe. Surviving in the other dimension is not. They are realms of existential extremes within an environment where the laws of physics can be bent as easily as a newly planted sapling."

"But what about…" Craig started to ask.

"I think we should leave it there," Ahote interrupted. "We've been through enough over the last few days – especially you. Focus your thoughts on reuniting with your family. Though I must stress that you must not talk of this with them. You remember Jenny being taken and thus her having knowledge of what occurred, but we changed the past. She has no awareness of anything unusual happening in your home. To her, you have simply been at work and are returning after a tiring day. To attempt to explain what has really occurred will only lead to friction and possibly even psychiatric treatment for you. What you have been a part of must remain in here."

Ahote tapped Craig's forehead.

"There should be no secrets kept from one's family, but this one is the exception to that rule," Ahote added.

The voice of the captain instructing the crew to prepare for landing ended the conversation. Craig wanted to ask more but knew that Ahote would not return to that subject.

The 747 descended into the smog-filled skies over Los Angeles. They crossed over the jammed 405 freeway then touched down with barely a bounce.

Craig donned his winter coat as they deplaned, expecting the weather to match what they had experienced in the UK. He was stunned to find Los Angeles sweltering in a rare January heatwave. It was expected to reach close to one hundred degrees.

They retraced their steps back to the SkyWest desk on the other side of the airport. They only had a two-hour layover this time and were soon boarding the commuter aircraft. After the luxury and spaciousness of the jumbo jet's first-class compartment, the cramped cabin of the Embraer turbo prop was something of a shock. Craig felt a momentary wave of claustrophobia attempt to hijack his rational thoughts. He closed his eyes and deep-breathed until the sensation had gone.

They landed in St George just as the sun was dipping behind the red cliffs. As they stepped onto the tarmac, Craig shivered. Not from stress but from cold. St George was sixty degrees colder than Los Angeles. He was glad he was still lugging around the heavy coat.

They found Ahote's Jeep exactly where they'd left it which, considering that St George had almost no crime whatsoever in 1996, shouldn't have been much of a surprise. The drive back was uneventful. Darkness had descended on the high desert so there was little to see outside. They passed through the somewhat creepy town of Cathedral City then saw no other lights until they reached the outskirts of Fredonia.

Once they turned onto 89A, it was only eight miles to the Old Mesa Road turn-off. Craig felt elated and nervous at the same time. He had risked his own life to save his family. He felt like a returning warrior, but accepted that nobody would ever know what had transpired. Jenny would perhaps think him a little distracted, but the kids would be completely clueless. The strangest thing would be the following day when he drove off to work and carried on his fulfilling, even if slightly mundane, life. Then again, after what he had just been through, mundanity would do just fine.

He was brought back from his musings as Ahote turned on his turn signal then guided the Jeep down the road that shouldn't have existed.

CHAPTER
TWENTY-SEVEN

They drove in silence along the hard-packed road. The night was completely clear. As they rounded the final curve, Craig could see Ahote's shack.

"When are you gonna do whatever it is you do so that I can get back to 2021?" Craig asked.

"I just need about fifteen minutes of complete quiet to reset my timeline."

"You make it sound so easy," Craig commented. "What do you do, chant or something?"

"Do you want me to chant, Craig?" Ahote asked him sarcastically. "I don't need to, but if chanting would help, I'm more than happy to do so."

"I'll just shut up and let you do your thing."

"Thank you," Ahote smiled.

They pulled up in front of the shack and stepped inside. It was cold. When they were last there, a fire had been burning giving the small room some badly needed heat. Without warmth, the little shack seemed to have lost its previous charm.

"Have you ever considered putting in central heating?" Craig asked.

"No. But if you're that cold, we can wait till I get a fire going before I start the meditation?"

"Are you aware that you seem to be snapping at me since we got here?" Craig pointed out.

Ahote stood silently for a moment. His head lowered to his chest.

"I am sorry. I have no reason to bark at you. You have done everything that was asked," Ahote said.

"Then what's wrong?"

"You will think me a weak and vain man, but in my real time I am old and suffer from all that that entails. For the past few days, I have been twenty-five years younger and felt what it was like to not ache with every movement. To not become breathless after the slightest exertion. I am about to step back into a far older body that doubtless doesn't have that many seasons left in it."

"I'm sorry, Ahote. I never gave that any thought." Craig nodded his understanding.

"Nor should you. It is not your concern."

Craig was about to argue the point when Ahote interrupted him.

"Let me complete the timeline reset so that you may go home."

Craig mimicked closing a zipper across his mouth. Ahote sat in his chair and closed his eyes then began Ujjayi deep breathing. Within less than a minute Craig could see the other man's facial features relax and go slack.

Ahote sat in that position for twenty minutes without any movement other than the slow rising and falling of his chest. He then slowly opened his eyes.

"You should go home now and see your family," Ahote announced.

Craig noticed that the man had aged during the meditation. He was back to looking like the old man who had originally appeared at his accident site in Glendale.

"You look old," Craig stated. "I'm sorry."

"I have simply returned to my correct place in time," Ahote said.

"Why did you get younger and I stayed the same?"

"Because I was revisiting my own timeline therefore in 1996 I looked as I had looked in 1996. You, however, were only a guest and remained as you now are."

"One day you're going to have to go into a little more detail about that," Craig said.

"Are you suggesting we will be seeing each other again?" Ahote smiled.

"No… I just meant…" Craig stammered.

"I know what you meant. You should go now."

"That's it?" Craig asked in amazement.

"That's it." Ahote rose slowly from his chair. "You still need to walk back to your vehicle. Once you pass through the mist, you will have returned to your time."

Craig was at a loss for words. He felt that there were a million things to say but at that moment he couldn't think of one of them.

Ahote smiled as if knowing what Craig was thinking. "There is no need to say anything. Our actions have negated the need for words."

Craig nodded his understanding. "Will I ever see you again?"

"I don't know the future. I have a feeling that we might, but that side of my timeline has yet to unfold for me."

Craig took one last look at the old man then stepped out of the shack. It was surrounded by fog. It was dense but Craig could just make out the path to the dirt road. He followed it, carefully making sure he didn't stumble into any of the deeper ruts. As he walked further away from Ahote's shack the fog became even thicker and all he could do was look straight down and make sure that each footstep remained on the road.

Then, without warning, he stepped out of the grey mist. His county sheriff's vehicle was where he'd left it. He opened the driver's door and was almost startled as the dome light came on. He noticed his cell phone still sitting in the utility well between the front seats. He pushed the home button and it lit up.

Craig pressed his speed dial for home but saw that he had no cell service way out there in the middle of nowhere. He drove back along the road till he came to Messy Rock. He grabbed his Maglite and eased out of the SUV. He walked around the boulder and shined the light up to the ledge. He could clearly see his carvings.

He returned to the Explorer and drove on till he reached 89A. He turned right and headed towards Kanab. He kept checking his phone signal. Three miles from town, he was in range of one of the hilltop repeaters. He pulled over and hit redial.

After three rings Jenny answered. "You're early? Are you headed home already?"

Craig couldn't talk. The wave of emotion was unexpected. Tears streamed down his face. "Honey, you okay?" Jenny asked.

"Fine. Sorry about that."

"You sound like you have a cold."

"I had to spend some time off road today. It's allergies," he fibbed.

"We just got back from picking up Steeler from the groomer. You should hurry if you want to see what she looks like all clean and brushed," Jenny said.

"I love you, you know," Craig announced.

He could hear Jenny start to laugh. "I don't know what that was for but I love you, too."

Craig heard Sally say 'yuck' in the background.

"I'll be there in ten," Craig said before disconnecting the call. He couldn't believe that they were okay. That nothing from another dimension had entered their home and destroyed their lives.

Craig looked up towards the heavens and mouthed the words 'thank you', then put the SUV in gear and headed home. As he passed through the south end of Kanab he saw the new hotels with their brightly illuminated, branded frontages and took a deep breath. He really was back.

He turned east on HWY 89 and drove the twelve miles to the Johnson Canyon Road turn-off. As he rounded a bend in the road he could see all the house lights and even the smoke rising from the chimney. He felt another wave of the earlier emotion but managed to keep it in check. He couldn't walk into the house blubbering. To them he had only been gone eight hours and even then they thought he was just twelve miles down the road. They didn't know, nor should they ever know, that he had been 6,000 miles and twenty-five years further away.

He drove up their packed dirt drive and into their gravel forecourt. He could see into the kitchen window and saw Sally and Tim playing at the kitchen table. He couldn't immediately see Jenny, then the utility room door opened and she was standing there smiling. The light from the room back lit her hair so that it almost looked golden. Steeler stood next to Jenny and was looking anxiously up at her. She patted him on the head then whispered, "Go to Daddy."

Steeler shot out of the door and charged at Craig. Inches before colliding with him, Steeler turned sideways and did his crazy 'happy to see you' wiggle. Seeing such goofiness from such a big dog always made Craig smile.

The two of them walked to the door and stepped into the house.

Craig took Jenny in his arms and held her tight as Steeler flopped onto his back right on top of Craig's feet.

"What's gotten into you?" Jenny teased as she looked into Craig's eyes.

"I just missed you, is all," Craig replied.

"I missed you too," she replied shaking her head and grinning at Craig's unexpected affection. Jenny started to put Steeler's nightly kibble in his bowl. He practically levitated to his feet then buried his snout into the chow and started to scarf them down.

Jenny and Craig left him to his meal and walked into the kitchen.

"How are you two doing?" he asked as Tim and Sally turned to face him.

They both had handfuls of Lego blocks but managed to nod signifying that all was well.

"Go change and put your stuff away then I'll start dinner," Jenny said.

Craig hadn't noticed that he was wearing his sheriff's uniform and utility belt that he wore at work. "That can wait. I'm starved," he announced.

Jenny gave him a theatrical glance down to his holstered Glock.

"Sorry," Craig nodded.

As he put the gun in the safe, Jenny put breaded cod steaks in the oven for them and fish fingers for the kids. She then grabbed a glass from the cupboard and retrieved an O'Doul's Amber from the fridge.

Craig listened to the kids tell him all about their day's adventures then Jenny updated him on a few home matters.

"I don't know what made me think of it but I had your Aunt Gina on my mind today. Do you ever hear from her?" Craig asked casually.

"That's funny you should ask. I got a call from her this morning. She was feeling a bit blue," Jenny replied.

"Why?" Craig asked trying hard not to show the joy he was feeling.

"It's the twenty-fifth anniversary. It's not unnatural that she'd feel sad."

The chill exploded at the base of Craig's spine.

"Twenty-fifth anniversary of what?" He tried to keep his voice calm.

"You know, honey. That was when her daughter disappeared." Jenny seemed surprised at her husband forgetting that. Aunt Gina got into a terrible funk every year at that time.

Craig slowly rose from the table.

"Honey?" Jenny looked worried.

"Stay in here. All three of you – please."

Craig slowly walked out of the kitchen and into the hallway. He took a few steps towards the living room until he could see the wall on the right.

He felt as if the sturdy stone floor beneath him had turned to quicksand. He couldn't catch his breath. He stepped into the room and faced the ancient mirror that hung on the wall.

"Oh, by the way, we really need to get the animal guy over here. The sounds from the attic have been getting worse all day," Jenny called out from the kitchen.

Craig's hand dropped to his holstered Glock. It of course wasn't there. He looked carefully at the mirror. It appeared to be the same one they'd initially received. He tapped the end of his finger against the reflective surface. It sounded and felt like a mirror should. He backed up till he had a full view of the antique looking glass.

"You guys put on your coats and go outside till I tell you to come back in," Craig called out.

He took one more step backwards till he could feel the curtain from the patio door behind him. He smelled something familiar. He had last smelled it at the cottage in England. It was the smell of something earthy yet rotten. It was coupled with the odour of ozone that you get during a lightning storm.

Craig slowly turned to the curtain. He slowly drew back the material.

There was nothing there.

He turned back to the mirror and froze. Beyath was less than a foot away from him. He could see the recognition in her face. Her jaundiced eyes seemed to twinkle as the leathery skin around her mouth formed into a hideous grin. He tried to charge her but couldn't move. He tried to swing his arm at her but still couldn't move. He realised that he was in the same type of trance as his children had been when he'd last seen them. He was riveted to the spot. Even his eyes were locked facing forwards.

While she continued to stare at Craig with an expression of deranged amusement, she opened her mouth and spoke. The words that came out of her were Craig's words, in Craig's voice.

"You guys can come back in now," Beyath shouted, sounding exactly like Craig. "Everything's okay in here."

The kids ran in first. The second they reached the living room they froze in place. Both children suddenly rose a few inches above the floor and glided across the room to the sofa. They then settled back to the ground and sat on the sectional in almost the exact position Craig had found them the first time.

Jenny walked into the room. "What the dickens was all that about? I thought you'd…"

She saw Beyath and amazingly, her first instinct was to try and attack the creature. She only managed to get a few feet before she too succumbed to the witch's spell.

Beyath faced the mirror and in a raspy, time-worn voice said, "Veita." The surface of the mirror rippled and became opaque. Jenny rose a few inches above the ground and began to float towards the mirror. Craig saw everything but was unable to help his wife in any way. He might as well have been a block of concrete for all the good he could do.

Beyath walked into the opaque glass with Jenny floating only inches behind her. The moment she passed through, the mirror suddenly shattered, its reflective shards crumbling to the living room floor.

Craig suddenly screamed "No!" It shook the house to its foundations. He felt his world tip and was plunged into complete blackness.

Craig was standing back at the gun safe. He was about to lock the combination as he'd done a few minutes earlier. He immediately flashed back to Iraq and the déjà vu he thought he'd experienced before the roadside bomb blast. He realised it wasn't déjà vu at all. It was something else. Something extraordinary.

He retrieved the gun and ran into the living room. He again stepped to the curtains and flung them open. He knew she wouldn't be there.

"Who's my goofy boy?" Craig yelled at no one, then turned. Beyath was directly in front of him as before. She had the same demonic smile, the same odour of rot.

Craig started to raise the gun but froze. He tried to lift the other hand but couldn't. Beyath was about to call the family into the room but noticed something very strange. Even for her. Craig was under the spell and couldn't move, but he was smiling. Even in her ancient and obviously insane mind she couldn't understand the smile.

She took a step back.

Then Craig heard what he had hoped he would. It was a gentle rumbling that was growing louder by the second. Beyath heard it too and her mummified features looked momentarily puzzled until 120 pounds of yellow Lab slammed into her legs. She did a complete somersault then landed in a crumpled pile on the ground.

A lot of things happened at once. Beyath rose back to her full height, Jenny stepped into the room and Craig, momentarily free from the trance due to Beyath's encounter with Steeler, fired off two shots. Both hit Beyath. One in the neck, the other in the chest. She howled at such a piercing volume that the windows and doors of the old house rattled in their frames.

She fell to her knees and managed to grab hold of the bottom of the frame. She started to pull herself through the portal. Craig took aim and was about to finish the job when Jenny stepped in front of him.

"Stop. What are you doing?" Jenny sounded horrified.

Craig didn't have time to argue the point and took a step sideways to give himself a shot. Jenny mirrored his move and continued to block him.

Beyath was now more than halfway through the shimmering portal when Steeler grabbed her by the ankle and dragged her screaming, halfway back into the room.

"Steeler! No!" Jenny yelled. He released her leg and she tried again to crawl back to her other dimension.

Ahote's voice suddenly filled the room.

"Veita!" he yelled.

The room was filled with the sound of glass cracking.

Ahote stepped into the living room and looked down at Beyath's lower half protruding from the mirror. His command had closed the portal while she was still trying to get across. Her legs twitched twice then went still. The mirror had formed perfectly around her.

"Is everyone all right?" Ahote asked as he looked to the others. The kids looked terrified as they poked their heads around the corner. Jenny was opening her mouth wide, trying to clear her ears.

"That gun is really loud," she stated. She looked at Ahote with a puzzled expression.

"You're the man who came to our door a few nights ago."

"I am indeed, Mrs Edmonds."

Craig patted him on the shoulder. "Good job he decided to come back. Actually, why did you come back?"

"I thought it would be a good idea to check up on Gina's health. I called Edward and heard about Gina's daughter."

"Yeah," Craig nodded. "I heard the same thing. Beyath was waiting for me. I don't know why she didn't kill me."

"Leaving you with a lifetime of pain and anguish was far more preferable to someone like her."

"What the hell are you two talking about!?" Jenny asked.

"Mommy said a bad word," Tim giggled.

Jenny grabbed one of the throws from the back of the couch and threw it over the remains of the witch.

"Guys, let's go into the kitchen the long way. There's glass on the floor by the mirror."

She stepped over the throw and led the children out of the double doors to the deck. As she passed Craig she threw him one of her 'now what have you done?' looks.

"You both have some explaining to do," she stated as she ushered the kids out of the room.

"What do we do about this?" Craig asked gesturing to the two feet sticking out from under the colourful throw.

"A clean-up crew is on their way from Las Vegas as we speak. I suggest that you take your family to one of those wonderful new hotels in town and spend the night there. I believe most of them accept pets."

"I don't know what to say." Craig shook his head. "Thank you."

"I don't think I deserve the credit here," Ahote advised. "Between you and Steeler, I wasn't left with that much to do."

"How did you know about the command for the portal?"

"I heard it when I was hiding behind Gina's sofa in England," he admitted.

"I thought you couldn't get involved and alter the outcome?" Craig recalled.

"Only when I have stepped back into my timeline. When I'm in the present, I can get into whatever mischief I please."

"Well, you've certainly done that tonight." Craig smiled. "I'd better get my family out of here. Will you be all right?"

"Me? I'm always all right."

Craig laughed as he headed for the kitchen.

Ahote lifted one end of the throw and stared down at the half corpse. He sank to the floor and sat cross-legged as he began the Kachina ceremony to rid the space of the *Buaka*.

The next morning, while his family was still asleep in the comfort and safety of their Hampton Inn room, Craig crept down to his SUV and drove south on HWY 89A.

He turned left onto Old Mesa Road and after a mile saw Messy Rock coming up on his left. He slowed down as he approached the road closure signs. He stopped and walked the last few feet. The road no longer existed. In its place was a ten-foot drop where rushing water had eroded everything in its path.

No vehicle could ever drive any further on that road.

At least not then.

EPILOGUE

Months later, under the shadow of Australia's famed Ayers Rock in the northern province of central Australia, the girls had just finished making camp under the supervision of their two team leaders.

As the sun began to set behind the massive red rock that the Aborigines call Uluru, it began to change colour. Its daytime rust-red hue transformed into light then dark purple as the daylight gave way to nightfall.

The girls knew how rare it was to obtain permission to camp next to the famous landmark, long considered a sacred site to the Aboriginal people. They had been granted the honour as they were the first all-Aboriginal Girl Guide team in Australia. They had been camping for seven days in various locations throughout the country. Their last night was to be spent under the stars only feet away from Uluru. It was to be the highlight of the trip.

As well as the eleven girls and the two team leaders, there was a two-person documentary crew following the campers throughout their historic journey.

One of the team leaders, Killara Mears, was the daughter of an Aboriginal father and a Swedish mother. Her face with its strong Aboriginal features was topped with a mane of curly blonde hair. Her blue eyes were piercing and were a window to the intelligence behind them. She had worked for the Guides for three years and had been one of the strongest proponents for creating an all Aboriginal team. Despite early opposition to the idea from the press and the Guide leadership, Killara managed to assuage their concerns about taking a step backwards in the battle for diversity. She made clear that the team would not be a permanent all Aboriginal unit, rather one that would form every three to six months and help young Aboriginal women and girls to fully understand the ways of their ancestors and be able to immerse themselves in their geographic and ancestral history throughout Australia.

The other leader was not Aboriginal. Alice Straight was in her forties, lived almost every day of her life outdoors and had an uncanny resemblance to the character, Crocodile Dundee. She had been with the Guides for over twenty years and was the team leader that every girl wanted to have as their guide into the outback.

The leaders tried to leave most of the chores to the Guides as the girls were there for the experience. They watched as three of the older girls gathered some brush and dried wood to make the campfire. Others helped dig a pit and line it with stones. They had made sure to not build it too close to Uluru so that it wasn't blackened by smoke from the flames.

Once the fire was going, Alice stepped in and took over as camp cook. While ancestral tradition in the bush might have been for them to eat goanna and witchetty grubs, Alice was also known for her ability to create what she called 'bonza trail tucker'. The team had eaten incredibly well for the whole week but that night, Alice was going all out. That night they would eat pasta with wild mushroom and fennel followed by a flourless dark chocolate cake made in a frying pan over the open flame.

The documentary predator (producer/editor) was also the camera person while the second crew member was responsible for sound. Both women had won awards for their work and had been chosen for this assignment because of the respectful way they told their stories. The girls and their leaders loved the fact that the crew was almost invisible. They were never 'in your face' or interrupted meaningful moments just to jump in with a question or an intrusive camera angle.

The pair had decided to record the group at the base of Uluru but from a distance. They found a rocky outcrop that offered a view that was angled down on the gathering. It gave a wonderful sense of the camaraderie against the back drop of the dramatic and remote landscape.

They sat silently and recorded as the team leaders explained some of the spiritual beliefs associated with Uluru. One of the younger girls stepped forward with a handful of berrigan emu bush leaves and threw them onto the fire. She was performing the Aboriginal smoking ceremony which is used to ward off evil spirits. They all watched as the smoke rose into the air. The camera captured the young women as they bowed their heads in respect for their ancestors.

As the documentary team looked on, they saw the fire turn blue. They assumed that it must have been a reaction to the leaves. Then the smoke turned jet black. The Guides and their two leaders seemed to be enthralled by the unusual behaviour of the campfire. A few of the girls were even giggling.

Something about the density of the smoke caused the laughter to stop. A strange odour began to permeate the air within the campsite. It smelled like ozone; a little like the electric smell that accompanies a violent thunderstorm.

The campers backed away from the fire as if sensing that something was wrong. They all saw part of the black smoke suddenly separate from the rest. Instead of rising into the night sky, it hugged the barren earth as it crept away from the fire. It stopped and seemed to wait for the rest of the ground-hugging smoke to catch up and form into a six-foot-wide black circle.

The leaders called for all the girls to gather behind them as the black smoke began to rise from its centre and form into some sort of shape. It was no longer smoke. It began to solidify and grow upwards. The blackness was soon over seven feet tall. It looked like a giant black cactus until more detail began to form within the shapeless mass.

The first recognisable thing were the eyes. At least the onlookers assumed they were eyes. Each was an identical vertical slit about three inches long. There were four of them equidistantly covering a rough orb shape that had formed at the top of the entity. Within the slits, marble-like eyes, or whatever they were, seemed to be a shade of red that was impossible in nature.

The next recognisable thing were the teeth. Below the eyes, a mouth had formed. It stretched across one entire side of the thing. Almost a third of the creature's height was taken up by the gaping maw. The rows of pointed teeth filled the orifice. In the centre, a thin purple tongue flicked out as if tasting the night air.

The young girl who had thrown the leaves into the fire stepped away from the others and shouted at the towering mass.

"We're not scared of you. You can't hurt us. The spirits of our ancestors will protect us."

The utter blackness then moved towards them.

Tim and Sally had gone to bed hours earlier. Jenny and Craig had just finished watching a cheaply-made horror film on Netflix. Despite the low cost of the production, the film about a girl getting trapped under a flooded house infested with alligators had been able to illicit quite a few muffled screams from Jenny and even a couple of leg jerks from Craig. As Jenny headed for the kitchen, Craig turned to CNN to catch up on the day's news before bed. He used to be able to do it in the early evening but with two young children in the house and having no idea what new horrors were to be reported, it turned into a late-night tradition.

The impeccably made-up and over-quaffed female anchor was in mid story about a Girl Guides group that had vanished while on a camping trip to Ayers Rock in

Australia. The image of Uluru was in the top right corner of the screen. The reporter took up the rest of it.

The police apparently had no clue as to what had occurred. All that was left was their carefully prepared campfire stones and some ash left over from the blaze. There was rumour that a video crew had been travelling with the group to film their adventure for a future documentary. No trace of the camera or the crew could be found. Their disappearance was currently a complete mystery.

Craig couldn't help remembering Ahote's words about unsolved disappearances. He hoped this one wasn't going to fall into that category. However, the chill that was starting to form at the base of his spine said otherwise. He told himself that the chill meant nothing. People went missing all the time and turned up perfectly safe. The campers probably just moved on or something.

"Honey?" Jenny called from the kitchen.

"Yeah," he called back distractedly.

"Did you know that Ahote is standing outside the house? He's on our driveway."

The chill had been right. As if in celebration of its premonitory ability, it crawled up the rest of his spine.

"What's he doing?" Craig asked.

"I don't know but if I had to guess, I'd say he was waiting for you."

Craig took a couple of relaxing breaths then headed for the front door. He opened it and saw Ahote standing about twenty feet away from the house.

"I didn't want to wake the children," he spoke softly.

"This is about those other children, isn't it?" Craig asked, already dreading the answer.

Ahote's eyes met Craig's. There was something new in them. Something that Craig never expected to see in his friend's eyes.

He saw fear.

For exclusive discounts on Matador titles,
sign up to our occasional newsletter at
troubador.co.uk/bookshop